T0103493

THE DEATH STORY

THE DEATH STORY

AMAY SAXENA

PARTRIDGE

Copyright © 2016 by Amay Saxena.

ISBN: Softcover   978-1-4828-8633-7
               eBook   978-1-4828-8632-0

All rights reserved. No part of this book may be used or reproduced by any means, graphic, electronic, or mechanical, including photocopying, recording, taping or by any information storage retrieval system without the written permission of the author except in the case of brief quotations embodied in critical articles and reviews.

Because of the dynamic nature of the Internet, any web addresses or links contained in this book may have changed since publication and may no longer be valid. The views expressed in this work are solely those of the author and do not necessarily reflect the views of the publisher, and the publisher hereby disclaims any responsibility for them.

Print information available on the last page.

To order additional copies of this book, contact
Partridge India
000 800 10062 62
orders.india@partridgepublishing.com

www.partridgepublishing.com/india

ACKNOWLEDGEMENTS

Just wait for few minutes, if you're thinking this only my book. People around me helped me in many ways.

So, I would like to thank people who showed faith in me and stayed by my side while I was penning down this book. In particular, I would like to thank:

My mother (Rekha Saxena) for her unflinching love! My dad (Niraj Saxena) for making me believe in my dreams and letting me do what I dreamt of! My brother (Ashish Saxena) for not disturbing when I was writing (Just Kidding).

Well, I have two more members in my family. My dogs—Chinu and Babu. They strolled around me, when I used to write during night. Really, they did not let me feel alone.

My friends, for criticizing me, motivating me, supporting me, and for helping me to transform into a better human being. Without them, this book would not have been reality.

Shruti Nair, my motivation and inspiration. Whenever I felt dejected, she chatted with me. I'm really going to miss her talks and her ways to make me feel better.

I'm thankful to god for giving me this talent of— telling stories and for his love and blessings.

The entire team of Partridge Publication for answering my crazy questions and cleared all my queries.

Finally, thanks to you all, for picking up this book. I hope you enjoy the story. ☺

Amay Saxena
2016

PROLOGUE

It would have been like any other night if my parents had not cancelled their plan to come back from Shimla. Things would have been different if there was not an empty compartment on train from Kalka to Mumbai. I would have never got my first book if I had slept earlier. Well, I had no control over it. My coincidental meeting with a woman (whom I have never seen yet found interesting), she narrating me a story and I'm happily listening to it. All the things, I mentioned don't happen even rarely. It was all planned by god.

I had nothing to do. I was bored. Even though I was not hungry, I was munching potato chips while surfing on internet. I was alone in the compartment. My family booked tickets but then thought of extending their stay in Shimla. So, I had three more seats empty. I was not feeling sleepy. I had nothing to do. The only thing I was doing was cursing my college for conducting exams in January. Train stopped at a station. I tried to identify the station but I was not able to. It was too dark outside. I had one more seat empty exactly in front of my seat which my family had not reserved. I simply assumed in my mind, this seat is going to remain empty all night. After 5 minutes, a woman (more looked like a girl) opened the curtains and peeped inside. After a minute, she was completely inside with her 2 big bags.

Wow! Two bags one woman. She is definitely on a tour.

She settled herself in front of me after many attempts to put her bag under the seat. There were enough places to keep her both the bags on my father's and mother's seat still she was trying to make some more space. She was a beautiful woman with a cute face like a girl. In India, after a certain age extraordinarily beautiful women are called as aunties by teenagers like me. Even though they deserve some more respect for few more years. She was one of those. I tried to look at her to know that she was already looking at me. I smiled at her.

'Hello, beta' the unknown woman asked me.

'Hi, aunty' I answered.

'Where are you coming from? Are you all alone?'

'Yes and I am coming from Kalka.'

'You don't feel sleepy?'

'Yes. I am.' I lied and tried to sleep by covering myself with a blanket. No, I was not trying to hide myself from her. It was freezing temperature outside.

I acted like I was sleeping and from corner of the blanket I saw that aunty was not interested in sleeping. She was sitting, quietly. Why she wants me to sleep then?

I tried to adjust my blanket. She looked at me as if I had broken hostel rules.

'I don't think you want to sleep. You're wide awake.'
She said leering at my open eyes. Attractive eyes, I saw. I
got up and went to washroom. Indian Railways have made
air conditioned bogies but condition of washrooms is still
substandard.

'Are you not going to sleep all night?' asked the lady.
Stop questioning me, I wanted to say. I control myself.

'I don't know' I replied with a not so good expression.

'What is your name?' She asked me, again. A part of
me wanted to sleep for peace now.

'Amay Saxena'

'What's your name, aunty?'

'Nita Iyer' after this, she asked some basic questions
like college, courses, etc.

'This train is quite empty. How come you are travelling
alone?'

'Actually, I had done reservations for my entire family.
They cancelled their return plan and my exams are also
going to start soon so, I decided to return alone from
Shimla. We went for a vacation.' I smiled.

'I am also going to Mumbai for some personal work.'

Nita got a call. I looked away. I had no interest in
staring her. I tried to look outside but I could only see
darkness. I couldn't help in overhearing her conversation.
She was talking to her daughter. She was a mother. It was
hard to believe but still I digested the fact. Like every
mother—Nita was enjoying her conversation with her
daughter. During her conversation, I learned, her daughter
was 10 years old. Nita's daughter also had some drawing
homework which she has not done and was convincing her
mom for a holiday tomorrow. I looked towards Nita. She

was fair enough to be compared to milk. She disconnected her call after whole twenty minutes.

'My daughter never sleeps without me. She and her mood swings, I am unable to control but she is overloaded with cuteness.' Nita said about her daughter. I had not asked for an explanation.

'I understand. Once I was also a kid.' I said proving her correct.

'So, you are a writer?' I nodded.

'Why you write?' This was a hard question to answer. I was not specific about my writing goals. I was also confused about me becoming a writer.

'I am confused. I am also a career focused one. I just write because I like to tell stories.' She laughed. There were two possibilities behind her laugh: one, I was sounding funny and second she was actually laughing at me. I was feeling dejected. I did not ask her why she was laughing.

'You can also write while you are studying. There is no compulsion on focusing on any one thing.' She said.

'I know. I am just too young to choose any one thing in life. It is a mature decision. I mean decisions which includes career.' She nodded. Normally, I don't talk about my career with anyone. But that night was different I continued talking about my career planning with her and she also gave me advices about how to go about life.

It was midnight when I realized we had chattered non-stop for whole one hour. I had never being so friendly with a stranger.

'You want tea?' Nita asked me. Chilly weather, talkative woman and interesting night—plus a cup of tea, a perfect combination, I would say.

She had brought tea in her medium sized thermos flask.

'Usually, teenagers don't drink tea.' Everyone is not the same.

'I'm addicted to it.' She gave me a me-too smile. I had to smile back after all I was going to have her tea.

'Beta, don't you feel strange. Are you not afraid of me being an evil spirit? Just like you watch in movies...' She said, freakishly. What did she expect me to do?

I almost burst out laughing after hearing it. All she could saw was my laughing face. I did not stop laughing until she gave me a glare.

'I do believe in supernatural powers. But I don't think any woman who is dead will come and sit in front of me.' I said, keeping my mobile aside.

'It can happen with anyone. At night, anything can happen. Trust me; anything. Do evil spirits like me get any better time other than night for roaming out?' She said acting mysteriously.

'Don't try it with me. You also got a call from your daughter. You also gave me tips on my career. So game's over before you play...' I said staring her.

'Did you even notice my ringing mobile?' I tried to remember. I hadn't notice anything like that.

'So? It can be on silent mode.' I answered with a smile. She laughed. Her laugh was annoying me.

'Okay. You are not afraid of anything. You don't think any evil spirit can meet you.' I nodded.

'You don't fear anyone...huh?' She said and sat cross legged. I nodded.

'So I will scare you! I will tell you a story and at the end of it, I am sure you would be afraid of me.'

'What's the story about?' I asked. If it's a boring one, I would sleep.

'The story is about a woman who kills her husband.'

'Interesting' I thought, empty compartment, strange woman and something very strange which I'm not getting now, different, no? Well, everything about that night was different.

'So, you are listening to me?' Nita asked.

'Yes' I said, hesitating. What if I doze off?

That night, she told me a story about a woman who loved her husband and never wanted to kill him but ended up murdering him.

PART ONE

CHAPTER ONE

They both were extremely happy, for the first time not because they were together, the reason behind their smiles was their new home. Ashish had worked hard to build this house. He desperately wanted to build this house. He had dreamed a family with Neha in this house, which was going to be their first personally owned home. Before this, they only had lived in rented apartments. The house was on Neha's land. Neha's grandfather left it in his will, who died two years before. Neha was not the only person left in her family of Rajput's but, her grandfather decided to give that land to Neha.   Neha's parents died in a car accident when she was only 9 years. They both were young and healthy but destiny had something else stored for them. It came as a shock to Neha. Neha was small enough to understand such things. After her parent's death, Neha's aunty Kusum Rajput took care of her. Kusum was unmarried so; it was easy for Kusum to take Neha home. Neha, in her routine life forgot about her parent's death.

She was looking forward for a great career as a teacher. Neha was clever and beautiful which kept her on height. When she completed her BA, she met Ashish. It was love at first sight. They met in some mutual friend's party. Later began seeing each other, during which they found out, they were in love with each other. They planned to get married. Their marriage was simple. Neha had only her Kusum aunty during her marriage. Neha had overcome the difficult phase of her life and was all set to begin her new life with her husband, Ashish.

Ashish was a handsome man, who was intelligent enough to be a scientist. Bad luck, he could only be an owner of his three hotels. He came from a very selfish and rich family. Ashish's father had his business of clothes. Ashish's father wanted to see Ashish as a businessman only. He started telling Ashish from a very young age, how much he would study, but his future is Desai men's wear (shop's name). Ashish wanted to become a doctor. He told his decision of becoming to doctor to his father. His father refused him. He was immensely hurt when his father refused him. Next day, he told his father, he doesn't want to become businessman. His father told him, he has no choice but to obey orders of his father. Ashish left his house the next day and went to Rajasthan to chase his dreams.

Young Ashish thought it would be an easy journey to achieve his dreams but, it wasn't easy for him. He worked as a hotel manager in some hotel and started saving money. By the end of three years, he was able to save money enough money. Ashish emotionally thought, one day his father would come searching for him. But he never came. Ashish wanted to invest money somewhere. So, he invested all his money in hotel business. He had a good experience in working in a hotel. Hotel business also had good profitability and progress was natural. He took loan from the bank and started with a small place. This time his luck stroke better. Ashish's business started to progress with a great speed. Day by day, he was becoming richer. But the loan he had withdrawn was still remaining. One day, he purchased a lottery ticket and by luck he won it. Ashish was one of those people who wanted to become something else but ended being something else. Luck, he believed in. Finally, memories of poverty were behind Ashish. He opened two more branches and was earning well. One day, he met Neha; it was love at first sight. They married and was about to start a peaceful life. He believed he got a beautiful wife like Neha just by luck.

They both had a very difficult life. At a very young age, both of them had faced ups and downs in life. Mr. and Mrs. Desai—name plate read. Neha's heart smiled when she looked at it. There are some emotions which are indescribable.

'It is beautiful.' Neha said, entering their home. It's like dream coming true, Ashish thought. He nodded and kissed on her cheeks.

'Let me show you your house'

'It's ours' Neha defended.

'It is on your land. Basically, it is yours.' Ashish said.

'This house is registered in your name. Are you going to argue now?' Neha said glaring at him.

'No I am just telling.' Ashish said and backed off. Their house consisted of 5 bedrooms, two were on the ground floor and 3 were on the first floor. It was a furnished house. Ashish had tried to make use of the best quality. Their house had marble flooring in an artistic manner. Neha felt satisfied after seeing the whole house. Neha's dream had come true.

It was night time and romance time too. Ashish and Neha had dinner in a nice restaurant and had returned home. Neha had planned to change her job. She used to teach in a school and was now going to join private classes as a history teacher. She had a good experience of 3 years and her teaching skills were undeniable. After a long time, there was only happiness in her life. She maintained a diary. She opened her diary and started to write in it.

> Today is the happiest day of my life. I and Ashish, from now onwards are going to live in our own house. No rented apartments, anymore. We both had this dream. Thank you god, you fulfilled it. I just don't want anything more from my life.

'Darling, what are you writing?' Ashish asked as he came inside their bedroom. Neha closed her diary and turned around.

'I am just completing my diary. It needs to be updated.' She said with a smile.

'Isn't it amazing? We are at our own house.'

'Words can't describe my feelings. I feel like jumping on the bed. Then I think Oh! I am so crazy about this house thing. Really this is special.'

'Anyways, it is all because of your grandpa. So, you did bring something in dowry, right?' Ashish said, laughing at her. Neha attacked him with a pillow.

'Stop okay! I am serious. If your grandfather had not given this land to you, this would have not been possible. A bungalow in such a posh area is hard to buy.' Ashish said and pulled Neha towards him and started caressing her hair.

'What's on your mind lover boy? Trying you luck.' Neha said removing his hand from her hair. Ashish did not say anything until his hands reached on her hips. She was now almost sitting on him.

'I don't need to try my luck, baby. That was before marriage. Now, I don't needanyone's permission.' Ashish said and kissed on her lips. They lost control over them within a minute and they were on bed. That night, they made love without caring about the world. Special steamy night, it was for them.

Neha got up before Ashish. Neha's face glowed in morning. Neha looked at Ashish with sparkling eyes. Ashish was sleeping tight. Tired Neha got up and went towards the washroom. 'I want to live my whole life with this man' Neha thought and went inside the washroom.

CHAPTER TWO

'You came home early?'

'Why can't I come early?' Ashish replied. Neha was cutting vegetables when Ashish came.

'You can come, of course. I want to tell you something.' Neha said and went towards the bedroom. Ashish followed her.

'Today when I came home, I was able to smell something very dirty. Like some rats were dead. It was a very dirty smell. I don't know what it was of?' Neha complained. Neha felt like vomiting when she came home.

'I can't smell anything, now' Ashish was feeling fresh. He did not have any work load today.

'The smell was there for only one hour, and then it was okay.'

'I think someone can be cleaning garbage nearby' Ashish tried to distract her mind.

'Maybe. Anyways, I have to cook. No time to smell.' Neha said and went out. Ashish kept himself busy counting number of notes he had earned today. Neha and Ashish both ignored the smell. Ashish kept his mobile on the dressing table and went to washroom. When he came back, his mobile was on the floor. It was strange but, Ashish decided to ignore it. Neha served the dinner. She called him up.

'Nothing special today' Ashish teased her. Neha hated it.

'No sir. Your same boring wife, with same boring dishes' Neha said showing her sarcasm. Ashish knew it well, it's not was not good to mess with Neha at night. Otherwise she would just launch into a lecture and whole night would be ruined. Ashish quietly ate his dinner. Even silences spoke a lot between them.

'You're washing these clothes, now. Baby, you should rest its late night.' Ashish saw her washing clothes when he entered the bathroom. Neha already was working during the day and she also made dinner for them. Ashish could see Neha was stressed. He cared for her as if she was a baby.

'No rest for your, baby. I have to read some lessons too. I have my history class tomorrow morning.' Neha said.

'No way, Neha, you need rest. Do one thing, skip this washing and read your lessons and sleep. Do it tomorrow.' Ashish said. Ashish went to bedroom to sleep. Neha sat with her book—The Last Mughal. She had more 50 pages remaining to complete it. Neha thought this was one of the most boring history books she had ever read. But she had no option but to read it. Job is irritating sometimes.

While Neha was reading the book, she heard a strange noise from the kitchen. She walked up to kitchen and saw one spoon was lying on the floor. Neha bend down to pick up the spoon, at the same time she heard a voice:

"Welcome"

Neha screamed. Neha had never heard such voice ever. It was a man's voice. Ashish arrived. He saw Neha in the kitchen and went towards her. Neha haven't recovered, yet.

'What happened?' Ashish asked her. Neha did not reply. At every next moment, Neha collapsed. Ashish was confused. Ashish picked up Neha in his arms and kept her on the bed. Ashish was not interested in sleeping anymore. He was panicked about what had happened? Neha was sleeping. Ashish tried to wake her up, but she did not respond. Ashish did not sleep whole night. Ashish needed some answers from Neha.

MORNING

Neha got up at 6 O'clock, with headache and pain in her back. She closed her eyes for few minutes and was trying to remember what had happened last night? She couldn't remember anything. Finally, Neha got up and she was surprised to see Ashish was awake. Neha gave him a quizzical expression. Ashish was in a serious mood. He was worried all night. Neha stood up, her legs were paining, her hands were shivering and she also had headache. Neha tried to smile at him.

'What happened last night?' Ashish's first question was. Neha wasn't expecting this.

'What?' Neha encountered.

'You should know it.' Ashish raised his voice. Neha's face turned off! Neha looked straight into his eyes, without a blink. Ashish's expression showed, he was extremely angry. Neha was unaware of everything.

'What should I know?'

'The thing which happened last night'

'What happened?' Neha had no answers to his questions.

'What's the last thing you remember?' Ashish asked Neha.

'I was reading my book, that's all I remember—after that I'm blank.'

'That's all. You were in the kitchen, unconsciously lying on the floor when I came out after hearing your scream. How you went into kitchen?' Neha shook her head. Her negative response, was irritating Ashish.

'I have a headache, Ashish. I am feeling weak.' Ashish came and touched her. Neha also had fever.

'Listen, I am not angry on you. But why you screamed? You must know it.'

'Ashish, I have answered it previously. I don't remember anything. That scream is important than me, no?' Neha said making a childlike face. Ashish melted faster than ice.

'I did not say that. Let it be. The best news is—you're okay.' He smiled and left the room.

Neha was confused about last night. Her memory system was acting unsupportive.

Neha had taken a leave from her classes. She was alone at home with strange thoughts darting her mind. She was trying to remember about that night. She was not able to. Smell of a dead body started spreading in the house. She sprayed room freshener. Suddenly, a sound came from her bedroom. Neha thought it must be a pigeon. She ran towards the bedroom and saw there was no one there. She was still able hear something. It was now clear as if someone was talking sitting there. Suddenly, some voice shouted in her ears:

"Leave your job."

Neha stepped back, horrified and screaming. She closed the door of her bedroom and searched for her mobile. She called to her workplace and said, 'I am quitting'.

She did not know why she quit the job? Just because that incident near, her bedroom or it was something else.

'Why you left your job?' Ashish asked her when he got to know about her decision.

Neha did not answer. She had no words. One night she opened her diary and started writing—

> I thought I was lucky to have such a life.
> I really was.
>
> My good days have come to an end, at every end there's a new beginning, I don't know what will it begin? I get depressed, suddenly, I get stressed suddenly, and I don't know what's happening with me. I feel alone, but I am not. I feel some strange energy inside this house.

Neha closed her diary and slept. Something bad was heading towards her and she was not ready for it.

CHAPTER THREE

The next morning, Suresh Bhatia (a businessman) was called for a meeting by his colony. He was a man who would torture you for his work and if his work is not done before time, he can kill you. He was one of the most irritable people on the planet. His nature reflected in his face. He had a dark complexion with a not-well shaped moustache, which made him look like some animal. But, talking about his positive points he was well-disciplined and punctual. He never liked if someone made him wait a bit more than five minutes. He was like a military man. Unfortunately, he became a businessman. He was on his way towards the Jai Ram colony office. He was a senior member of the society. It was one of the posh areas of Jaipur. Meeting started soon.

'Why this meeting has been called? No notice and all. What's so urgent?' asked one of the members. It caught the attention of the secretary Riya Rathod.

'I'll explain everything to you all. In our colony, the bungalow no. 33 was always closed. Many people said, it was haunted and there are many stories related to it. Some of the people in this room have experienced negative powers there when travelling at night. But, few days back, one couple (Desai's) has come to stay there. It's not that we did not warn them. We did. They did not listen to us. As I see, many people are saying there is danger to their life. I want this issue to be cleared today.' Riya said in firm voice. Even though she was a lady, she had good knowledge about how she has to handle various situations. Riya was a PHD in economics and had guts to be RBI governor.

'There is no solution to this. If they don't want to listen to us, what can we do? After all, that woman's land it is. They can do whatever they want. Let them die.' Mr. Bhatia said. Everyone inside the room looked at him as if he was a ghost. Riya gave him a sharp glare.

'No, we can't let anyone die after knowing what has happened there. We all have heard about it, right? We should go and make them understand. They are reckless not fools.' Riya said. Everyone in the committee started giving their own views. Suresh Bhatia was quiet all time. Riya was constantly observing him; she was surprised by his behavior. Finally, they all concluded to one decision.

'Tomorrow I and Mr. Bhatia will go to their home and will try to make them understand. Everything clear' Riya said and everyone was out of the room.

Riya saw Suresh in deep stress. She could sense that he was thinking something very carefully and accurately. Riya went towards Suresh and asked him:

'What happened?'

'Nothing' Suresh replied.

'What are you thinking?'

'Nothing'

'You're coming with me tomorrow?' Riya asked him.

'Of course' Suresh said and walked away.

He was thinking: what was going to happen if they continue staying there?

DESAI'S HOME SAME MORNING

Neha sat on the sofa reading newspapers. She was in the middle of some crime article when she realized someone was staring her from the bedroom door. She suddenly looked there, she could she Ashish was standing there. He was wearing his belt. Neha felt something strange. She was again lost in that newspaper article.

'Wife killed by her husband at home' Neha read out loud. This grabbed Ashish's attention. He came in the drawing room. He looked towards her.

'What was that?'

'Reality of marriage, always a woman has to be a victim.' Neha said with anger in her voice.

'Why are you saying this to me?' Ashish's response came very fast.

'You can also kill me.'

'Stop it. Your mind has become very negative, I don't know what's cooking in your mind? Why you left your job?' Ashish had asked her this question hundred times.

'I told you, I don't feel like working anymore. I want to rest.'

'No! No! Rest and make imaginary stories of me killing you.' Ashish shouted. Neha felt she was insulted.

'If you can't pay for my expense, then just say, I will join my job again.' Neha shouted.

'I am not saying that. I am just saying—don't be depressed and don't make me angry. Live peacefully.'

'Don't change the topic, my dear. I know once you men are bored with your wife's body you need someone else in your life.' Neha blurted.

'What do you mean? I have other affairs.'

'Who knows?' Neha said softly. Ashish's temperament went high. Neha's eyebrows shot up.

'I didn't know how cheap you're? Don't you have any shame?' Ashish's voice was touching sky.

'No!' Neha said and laughed aloud. Ashish was still angry.

'Why the hell are you laughing?' Ashish asked.

'I was just joking, baby! I know you will never leave me.' Neha stepped forward and kissed on his forehead. Ashish was now relaxed.

Ashish left after this and promised he would come early.

Neha closed the door and felt a strong shiver through her body.

Neha's mind quickly changed and she was blank. She couldn't remember – what had happened just few minutes back?

She went towards the kitchen thinking what she will make for dinner.

SAME DAY: AFTERNOON, 2.45 PM

Neha was ready to step out of the house. She had planned going shopping with her friends from Knowledge Classes (where she worked earlier). Just before she could step out of the house, doorbell rang—she went towards the door and opened it wide. There was no one. When she closed the door, there was again a ting-tong. She again opened the door, this time confused. Neha was already so stressed within her; she only needed a reason to get hyper. Finally, she was able to step out of the house. When she looked at the front after locking the door, she again heard doorbell ringing. This time she was the only person present there and she had not pressed the doorbell button. She feared looking back. She stood there silently for few seconds and then went outside the main gate of her bungalow. She heard some noise from the back of the bungalow. She went looking, there the noise came from? She was already terrified about what had just happened! The back side was fully clear. She moved towards the front, she passed the door and she noticed one thing there. There was a parcel kept on the front door. She looked everywhere but no one was at sight. She picked up the parcel. It wasn't really looking like a parcel. It was an old box, inside it, there was something, Neha could feel. She took the box inside and unpacked it. She found something very unusual from it. Something one could not send anyone. Neha was afraid of it. It was something which is common, but uncommon to feel or see. She got an old packet which had somebody's blood in it. This was it. Neha was never afraid of anything, but now she could be afraid of everything she sees or hears. There was an old piece of paper in the box. She unfolded it and she read in her mind:

Dear friend

This one is for you Mr. Rajput. Let's have some more fun, man.

Yours friend

Paper slipped from her hand. Neha wanted to know who had sent this. She had no means. Rajput—was her surname before marriage. Neha wanted to call Ashish but stopped herself because she thought he would blame her for this. What was it? Was this a sign of something bad? Neha's mind stopped working. Neha was confused. She decided to dispose this packet and paper. She went out and threw the box in the dustbin. She did not look back. Neha never wanted to see such day. Neha decided not to tell about this mess to Ashish.

Was her decision right?

CHAPTER FOUR

There was a knock on the door. It was Sunday, so Ashish had a holiday. He went and opened the door. Neha who was in kitchen came out. Mr. Suresh Bhatia and Mrs. Riya Rathod were standing at the door. They both were smiling looking towards Ashish.

'I am the secretary of this colony, my name is Riya and Suresh is a senior member of the colony. We both just wanted to have a chat with you both. Can we?' Riya said. Ashish nodded and let them come inside. Neha gave them glass of water each.

'What's the matter?' Ashish inquired. Riya and Suresh both looked at each other.

'It's a serious issue. You may have heard from someone, this land has experienced paranormal activities. Your neighbors had told you before the construction of house that this is not an ideal place to stay. Many old people had seen many strange things happen here. We want to request you something.' Riya said. Suresh was quiet.

'Request'

'Yes! We request you that you should shift from here.' Suresh was still quiet.

'I don't believe in evil and all. I just believe in god. Where should I shift from here? We don't have any other apartment. I have put lots of money to build this house.' Ashish said. 'This is her land' Ashish said pointing his hand towards Neha. All Neha could do was smile.

'We're telling you because this land is cursed. We're here for your betterment.' Suresh finally opened his mouth.

'Who had cursed this land?' Ashish asked, directly. Riya and Suresh shook their head. Later, Suresh said:

'This land has its own history.'

'What history?' This time it was Neha.

'We don't know much about this cursed land. Many years back something very bad happened here, very horrible. I only know an evil spirit stays in this land, only belongs to this land. Once you leave, it leaves you.' Riya said, seriously. Ashish chuckled. Riya did not know anything. She faked in front of them just to scare them.

'I don't believe. We have been staying here from more than a fort night, now. We did not experience anything. We didn't even see a woman in a white sari.' Ashish said and laughed on his own joke.

'It's not a joke Mr. Desai. There is a story related to this, that we don't know. Anyways, it's your choice. We came here to help you, anyways…' Suresh said, hurrying. Riya and Suresh both again gave their views and left. Neha went out and asked Riya:

'What can happen if we don't go from here?'

'Neha, something very bad will happen. Please.' Before Riya could complete Ashish called out for Neha. It was an incomplete conversation. Ashish was sure Riya and Suresh were over-excited. Neha came inside with anger filled in her eyes. Ashish had insulted their guest and Neha felt it wasn't right.

'What's up my darling?'

'You shouldn't have behaved the way you did. You were making fun of them.' Neha blasted.

'If they talk funny what one can do? Cursed land, really?' Ashish laughed again. Neha looked away from him and went towards the kitchen. Ashish realized he had hurt Neha. He followed Neha.

'Are you angry on your baby?' Ashish said in a baby voice.

'I am not angry on anyone. Leave me.' Neha said.

'By the way, what's the plan for today?' Ashish asked her.

'You make a plan. I will definitely participate.' Neha went inside the bedroom to keep something. She again smelled something bad. She looked outside the window and screamed. Ashish navigated her voice and came on the spot.

'Look outside the window' Neha cried.

Ashish looked out. He could see there was a dead dog inside their balcony.

'How he came here and who killed him?' Neha shook her head. He called the cleaner of the colony and told him to dispose the dead body of the dog. Neha looked frightened. Neha never had seen a dead body in her life not even of her mom and dad. Ashish and Neha cancelled all their plans and decided to stay home. Neha locked herself inside the bathroom and lots of questions encountered her mind:

Who kept the dead body of a dog in our balcony? Was the blood I got yesterday was of this dog? No! Is this place really haunted? What's next then?

Suddenly, a five alphabetical word appeared in her mind: DEATH. In response, she shouted, 'No'

She was feeling tired of herself.

She came out and slept without having a word with Ashish. Ashish found it, strange.

NEXT EVENING

Frustrated and tired Ashish came home early in not a good mood. Neha sensed his bad mood and smartly kept quiet. As Ashish entered the bedroom, the room smelled very bad. He was irritated by this. He called out for Neha.

'Yes?' Neha asked.

'This room just pongs of a dead rat. Did you clean this room today?' Ashish shouted.

'Yes of course I did. Before you came I sprayed ambi pur too. Still it's stinking.' Neha explained.

'This smell is making me insane. I can't handle it. Close this room we will sleep in another room.' Neha followed his instructions. Ashish left the room leaving Neha alone there. Neha took blankets and pillows with her. Neha was closing the door and she heard some strange voice saying:

"Don't come here. I will kill you!"

Neha screamed. Ashish heard Neha screaming and went towards bedroom.

'What happened?' Ashish asked her.

'I heard some saying, "Don't come here. I will kill you". I was just…' Neha stammered. Neha was scared.

Ashish opened the door of the bedroom and went inside. Ashish looked everywhere but he couldn't spot anyone.

'There's no one inside. You must have overheard. It's illusory, sometimes. Relax baby.' Ashish said and hugged her. Neha pushed him.Neha was confident about it. She had heard someone.

'No, Ashish. I heard it. I was alone here. Believe me. There is someone other than us in this house. What Riya and Suresh said is right.'

'So, you believe them. They are just overdoing their jobs. There is no one. This is all bullshit. I say you, don't believe in all this otherwise you will also be in trouble. It's all in your mind, Neha.' Ashish wanted her to be quiet and relax but she was doing opposite to it.

'Ashish, let us leave this house. I don't want…' Ashish broke in and shouted at her:

'Listen, Neha I don't think this house is haunted and I request you please don't ever think about leaving this house.' Neha looked away. Neha was disappointed but she was also scared.

When I am alone, I am not. When I am not alone, I am uncomfortable, Neha thought.

'Ashish let us sleep upstairs. I don't want to sleep here.'

'That's what I said few minutes back, baby.'

'I remember.' Neha said.

CHAPTER FIVE

It was 2am. Suddenly, Neha got up. Neha was shocked by such moment by her body. She wasn't feeling whole of her. She was not in her senses. Neha went to the store room with a smile on her face. There was no one with her, only mysterious silence surrounded her. She sat on the chair located in the store room. She sat there for 2 hours doing nothing.

"Wake up!" someone told inside the room.

Neha realized she was not in her bedroom but she was in the store room. She was surprised. She too did not know how she came here. When Neha was walking towards the door, scared and horrified. She saw something written in block letters on a wall. She turned and read: "ASPD". She was confused. She had never heard anything about ASPD.

Neha went and slept beside Ashish.

Neha had no idea why was all this happening with her.

NEXT MORNING

'What? I don't believe in all this. Ashish is right. You're just stretching some simple things. There are no spirits, anywhere.' Mukesh said making fun of Riya. Mukesh was Riya's husband. He was an up to date man with no enemies and of course he was an chemical engineer with some good brain. He loved Riya. For now, he was laughing at Riya's theory behind Neha's land.

'It's not about what you believe or I believe! It is about their lives. I have questioned many old residents here. They all say, one man used to stay here. He was very famous, no doubt. But he came here sometimes. I want to know who that man is and what his connection with this land is. People who knew him personally are no more. What should I do? You say.' Riya said and drank water. Mukesh was quietly observing her. *She is so bothered about everyone!*

'I lack words in this matter, Riya. I can't talk about things I don't understand, know or believe. Sorry, dear.'

'Anyways, I don't need your help. Suresh is helping me.'

'Suresh, the angry bull' Mukesh laughed. He had named Suresh as angry bull.

'Stop it.' Riya said and smiled.

'He is really a pain in the neck.'

'I know. But he is at least nice to me. He got angry on Ashish when he declined to leave that house.'

'Obviously, anyone would get angry if someone will tell them to leave their own house. It's like insult.'

'We had a valid reason.'

'But...'

'I know it's not an analytical argument. But still I feel bad.' Riya said as her face grew sadder.

'Anyways, best of luck. You are going to meet Neha, today, no?' Riya nodded.

The ringing bell caught Neha's attention. Neha was busy reading *Oliver Twistby Charles Dickens*. She went up and widely openly the door. Suresh and Riya were standing in front of her. They greeted her and came in. Neha was not shocked to see them. Actually, she needed them. Suresh kept his backpack on the table.

'What would you like to take? Tea or coffee?' Neha asked them.

'No formalities, please' Riya said, instantly. 'Please sit down, Neha'

'Look, I know Ashish won't listen to us. But, at least you believe us. Neha this land is haunted and many of us believe in it. We're not fools.' Suresh said in a loud voice. Riya looked at him, indicating to lower his volume of voice.

'I know this. This place is haunted, I know. I have experienced many mysterious things. Like door knocking, I also heard various voices saying something to me and yesterday hell happened with me. Let me show you both.' Neha said. Actually, she shouted.

Neha took them to the store room. They could see, ASPD was written in blood.

'Dear, this is something I have never seen. It's written in blood. When did you see this?' Riya asked Neha.

'Yesterday night'

'Who wrote it?' Suresh asked.

'I don't know.' Neha said with fear in her voice.

'Of course, you won't know. It's not blood, anyways. It is paint, red paint colour. Someone many years back, painted it. Who lived here before you?' Suresh said.

'No one, this land was vacant for last 15 years. It is newly constructed.' Neha replied.

'What?' Suresh and Riya said in unison.

'This land and now the house, both are haunted. I guess you leave this house as soon as possible. This is a cursed land.' Suresh said. Neha was confused about what to do?

'Neha, tell Ashish about this ASPD thing. I don't know what is the meaning of it? Tell Ashish about it and I am sure he will understand your concern.' Riya said.

'I don't know. He doesn't believe me.'

'Do you believe in it?' Suresh asked her.

'Of course I believe. That is the reason I took you to store room. I feel some strange energy around. As if someone is always looking at me when I am alone. I feel someone walks with me and observes my every moment.'

'You told all this to Ashish?'

'No. He won't believe.'

'Neha look. I don't want anything to happen to you and Ashish.' Riya said.

'Thanks for your concern, Riya. I am thankful to both of you. At least you are listening to me.'

'Please talk to Ashish'

'I will' Neha said and looked up. They both were observing her. Suddenly, Neha's eyes turned red.

'I think you should leave. I have some important work.'

They both left. Neha closed the door and ran towards the bedroom and was jumping madly. She was not mad.

'You saw her eyes?' Riya asked Suresh.

'No!' Suresh said.

'Neha's eyes were red like blood.'

'What are you babbling? Nonsense'

'I am speaking the truth.' Riya defended.

'Let's go home.' Suresh dismissed.

Neha was banging her head on the wall, slowly. It was not hurting her. She was alone muttering something. Neha looked up, again. She realized she has to make dinner. She did not remember anything.

Why was she dashing her head on the wall?

Someone inside the house had the answer.

CHAPTER SIX

'This must be done by the construction workers. They also did the painting work.' Ashish said, after looking at the wall of the store room which had ASPD written on it. Neha was already afraid to tell Ashish about it. But, Ashish took it lightly. He straight away blamed painters for this.

'Where we got so much of scarp from?' Neha questioned.

'I told them to clean this. But they did not. Bloody assholes; only know how to take money!' Ashish said, abusively. Neha looked at dirty store room, with fearing eyes.

'What does it means?' Neha said, with anger. Ashish was not looking at her.

'ASPD? I don't know.' Ashish said, calmly.

Neha was again, feeling the strange energy inside her. Without uttering a single word from her mouth she went to the kitchen leaving Ashish alone in the store room. She took a knife for there. She was running towards the store room as if demons of hell were behind her. She stood in front of Ashish. She gave him a glare.

'What happened to you? And why are you carrying this knife with you?' Ashish asked her. Neha started laughing as if something hilarious had been asked to her. Ashish kept observing her.

'Why are you laughing?' Ashish asked again. She laughed even louder.

'Neha' Ashish shouted. Ashish saw Neha's eyes were fully red as if it were painted with blood. He stepped back. 'Neha' Ashish said again.

Neha closed the door and looked at Ashish with a smile. Neha sat down on the floor.

'Neha, why are you sitting down?' Ashish asked. She did not answer.

Suddenly, in seconds, lights went off! Ashish screamed. Neha laughed. There was horror in his voice and Neha loved it.

'What the hell is happening here?' Ashish cried. Next one minute, there was pin drop silence. Ashish tried to move out of store room but, it was dark so he couldn't find the way. Neha laughed, again. Ashish was all quiet. Ashish felt as if someone was holding his hand.

'Ashish' Neha said.

'Yes Neha!' Ashish replied. He felt good.

'Are you okay, Ashish?'

'I am confused! I don't want to stay here, anymore. Let's move out.' Neha laughed.

'Why the hell are you laughing?'

'When I told you earlier you did not took it seriously and now you want us to leave.'

'Neha…' She broke in.

'I am not Neha. I am Kumar.'

'What?' Ashish said. 'Why are you here for?' Ashish's hands were shivering.

'I am here to kill, everyone I know.' Someone from Neha's body replied.

'What?' Ashish shouted. 'Neha…'

'Baby, I am here only. HAHAHA…' reply came as.

'It's time to come back.' Neha said and forcefully stabbed the knife into Ashish's stomach. She attacked him again and again without even stopping for a minute. After five minutes, she stopped.

Neha collapsed on the spot. She remembered every bit of what happened, this whole incident only showed how powerful evil spirit was Kumar or someone else?

It was not Neha, who had killed Ashish.

Someone else killed Ashish.

CHAPTER SEVEN

Neha got up at 4am. She had a headache. She was already exhausted. She knew what she had done. Actually, she also knew she was possessed by a spirit named Kumar who did this. Neha had killed her husband. She felt it. She too wanted to die. Her lover was no more. Neha sat on the sofa with a bag of guilt in her mind and heart. Neha was feeling guilty and she had no answers to any of the question which were disturbing her mind.

Why is this happening to me? I never did anything wrong. Ashish, my love, my life and my world is no more. I killed him. I was the one who carried the knife to him. Lights went off! Why did I close that door? Why I killed him? Kumar, who the hell is he? I don't remember anyone called, Kumar. My life only has bad days. No good days!

Neha thought more than could.

She called her Kusum aunty and told her everything. Kusum told her, she would come as soon as possible.

The only thing Neha was doing was—cursing her. She switched on her laptop and typed in the Google search box—ASPD.

GOOGLE SEARCH

Antisocial personality disorder (ASPD) is a personality disorder, characterized by a pervasive pattern of disregard for, or violation of the rights of other.

Those with antisocial personality disorder (ASPD) are often impulsive a reckless, failing to consider or disregarding the consequences of their action.

People with this personality disorder will typically have no compunction in exploiting others in harmful ways for their own gain or pleasure.

Many people with this personality disorder have criminal records.

ASPD is considered to be among the most difficult personality disorders to treat.

There was more information about the disorder. She pressed herself to read everything about it. Neha had never heard about this disorder. Neha thought it wasn't related to her. But she wondered why it was written on the store room wall? Neha was feeling guilty, firstly and stressed, secondly.

"I could go to jail for killing my husband." Neha thought, discovering her future.

"No, I need to lie" Neha promised herself.

Kusum aunty came by 5pm; Neha explained everything to her once again. Kusum Rajput was almost on her keens after hearing everything. She was shocked. There were certain things, Kusum knew but never told to Neha.

"Neha needs to know everything, now" Kusum said to herself.

'Firstly, we need to clear Ashish's body. Main problem is we need to wait till the night and I don't think any more nights are safe here. We can't stay here.' Kusum told Neha. Neha already knew this fact.

'I don't want to go to jail. I did not kill him.' Neha confessed.

'I know, my dear. I just want you to know some talk about our family, which you haven't heard, yet. Some secrets related to this land.' Kusum said.

'Secrets? I want to know it, right now.'

'I also don't know.'

'Who knows it?'

'One close friend of your grandfather knows it.'

'Why was I not told about it, earlier?' Neha snapped.

'I don't know.'

'You knew I was shifting here, still… My god, I can't believe… Gosh' Kusum gave an angry look to Neha.

'We need to talk properly. Let's do it tonight after disposing the body. I hope you have enough guts to deal with the truth.' Kusum replied.

They maintained silence. *Silence, means problems too, sometimes.*

NIGHT

Neha and her aunty buried the body in the ground behind the bungalow. It wasn't hard. There was no one. Neha couldn't stop her tears. She knew she had to live her life, alone. Pain would be her companion.

"He died because of me." Neha thought and kept to herself.

'Put some leaves on it. So, no one will doubt. Anyways, we aren't going to stay here tonight. Let's move to some hotel.' Kusum declared. But, she was no one to declare, anything.

'Right. Let me change, first.' Neha said and moved inside the house. Kusum did not dare to step inside.

One hour passed, Neha didn't show up. Kusum was worried about her. She called her.

'Hello' Neha's response came.

'Where are you?'

'I'm dressing up'

'From one hour?'

'I'm coming.' Neha said and disconnected the call.

After 15 minutes, Neha came outside the house with a bag in her and locked the door. She wryly smiled at her Kusum aunty. Kusum did not smile back.

'Why it took so long time?' Kusum asked Neha.

'He possessed me.' Neha scoffed.

'What? Who? Kumar'

'No! This time someone called Rajesh.' Neha said, correcting her aunt. Kusum was horrified.

'How you know it?'

'He told me, he wants to kill me. I was out of my mind. I don't know I just got a scratch on my hand.' Kusum looked at the scratch. The wound was made by the blade.

'I think there are more evil energies. Are you okay?' Neha answered with a nod.

'What are you thinking?' Kusum asked Neha as they entered the hotel gate.

'Why he wants to kill me? If he wanted to kill me, then why did he first attack Ashish? And first of all, who is he?' Neha needed answers to all these questions.

'Why?' Kusum Rajput questioned and held Neha's hand showing her support.

Someone was there to haunt Neha.

CHAPTER EIGHT

Neha needed hope to keep her alive. Neha became a silent saint who had least interest in the world. Neha was afraid to face the mirror. She was afraid to face the world. She thought she was guilty. She became her own enemy. Neha started taking extra hot water bath which created redness on her fair skin. She became too hard on herself.

'So?' Neha said looking towards Kusum. 'We're here from 3 days. Where we have to go?'

'We're leaving today. We are going to Shimla to meet your grandfather's friend.'

'Why are we going to meet him?' Neha questioned.

'Because he knows what we don't. He knows that mystery.' Kusum said, angrily.

'What's his name?'

'Vikrant Gupta!'

'Who is he?'

'I don't know much about him. When I was small, he used to come to our house to spend time with us. I know that he knows everything about your grandfather.' Kusum asked, giving a suspicious look.

'I can talk with him on call.' Neha said rapidly.

'No. We will have to go. He is old...' Kusum said

'I'm sorry, I forgot.' Neha said. Kusum understood Neha was feeling fed up of her life. She had lost faith in everyone.

'Neha listen to me. I know what you are going through. I can understand your state of mind. Poisoning your thoughts won't let you live. This is not the end. I don't want you to be a booby lady who thinks she is a criminal. Fight for what matters to you the most. You can never change your past. You can only make your future better.' Kusum said, emotionally and understandably.

'Future without Ashish is blank.' Neha cried.

'Neha don't feel weak. Be strong and live.'

'You mean survive' Neha choked. Neha's life was empty without presence of Ashish.

Neha had faced many problems in her life. This one was the dangerous. All she was a, problematic woman.

Neha and Kusum reached Shimla by 9pm. They had a very quick air journey.

Kusum Rajput explained lessons she had learned her journey of life. Neha was quiet. Neha wasn't interested in her life lessons.

"She can all talk. There are no practical solutions in her lessons." Neha thought and drifted off!

They both ate at a hotel. Neha had no interest in eating but she had to survive.

After eating, Neha plonked her diary on the table and started writing:

It is unfair! Totally unfair. Whenever I try to be happy or feel happy, the thing which makes me happy is snatched away from me. This time it was my husband.

I feel no one.

I am no one.

Depressed Neha kept her diary back in her bag.

CHAPTER NINE

Vikrant Gupta aka detective Vikrant Gupta was living his retired life. He worked as a cashier in a bank, for almost 30 years. The permanent cashier got pension to live his life peacefully. Vikrant was also a secret detective and was working with the crime branch (police) in his earlier years. The reason behind, being a detective was a simple and sober one. He always said, "The cases which nobody can solve, I solve". That is why; he was the cleverest detective police ever had. Initially, during his detective years, he operated alone. One fine day, Vikrant met; Alok Rajput (Neha's grandfather), he saw himself in him. He was also clever. Vikrant needed Alok in his team.

"I want this man to work with me. We'll be the best of all." Vikrant said to himself. Vikrant approached Alok and discussed the work with him and to his surprise, Alok agreed instantly. For many years, both geniuses solved every case easily. They knew what was needed prior the investigation. Alok and Vikrant got many medals for solving cases, which police found harder to understand. Alok expired 2 years ago, leaving an unsaid note to his friend. Even if they were detective, they were best friends too because they found similar interest in them. Investigating and pulling out the truth, was their passion; not their job.

Vikrant Gupta had an amazing, thrilling and a good life. Now he was only waiting for his death and nothing mattered to him. Vikrant was washing his hand after his dinner when Neha and Kusum knocked his door. He knew they were coming. He also knew what they wanted? Kusum had already called him and told him they were arriving soon. He welcomed them and told the maid to bring two cups of tea for them and one cup of coffee for him. Neha tried to smile at him but she couldn't. Vikrant was old and classy in his way.

'I know you lost your husband. Trust me; it was not your fault, at all.' Vikrant said to Neha.

'When Alok died, I felt, a part of me was over. He was too close to me. The bonding we shared was beyond friendship. It was alike made for each other thing. I kept a deadlock for 3 weeks. I was shocked and livid. Anyways, I am okay now. An old man talk is boring right?' Neha was not here to get bored.

'I want to know everything about that land.' Neha ordered.

'There was a house there, earlier. Your grandfather and I operated from there. It was our office.' Vikrant told.

'Is there a story behind the supernatural powers I am experiencing?'

'Yes! I don't know about supernatural but, there's a story. Before I narrate, I want to know… What happened with you?' For the next one hour, Neha told him about what paranormal and ghostly incidents had happened with her. Vikrant was coughing continuously. Vikrant, however, was an old man, crying his problems to himself type of man. At this age, people get a bit lunatic. Vikrant went inside and came with a file.

'Isn't it fully covered with dust?' Kusum said. Vikrant ignored and opened the file.

'Why you brought this file, sir?'

'I will tell you later.' Vikrant coughed again.

'Neha, don't lose hope. Everything is going to be alright.'Vikrant said.

'You can start, sir.' Neha said and looked down.

Sometimes you just need trust yourself!

Neha found it harder to trust herself.

PART TWO

DETECTIVE VIKRANT GUPTA'S NARRATIVE—I

1972
Rajasthan

I exactly, remember the, day—it was Saturday morning. I did not notice date and time. I had taken bath and was having my first cup of coffee in morning. Usually, I have 3 cups, daily. I had no work and I was just going through the newspaper. These were my happy and tension free days, when I had no case to solve and bank had holiday on face. I thought of calling Alok over my place. I wanted to enjoy. Staying alone, isn't much fun? Although, Alok had his own family but he was naughty enough to give me some time from his, hectic schedule. Both of us had one thing is common; our passion to find out the truth. We loved it and we're lucky ones to have been following our passion from the last 5 year, together by wonder. The politics block had sucked up an area of brain, because of which I banged the newspaper on table and walked out.

Alok stayed three apartments away from me. Alok always had a shy grin and never was enough confident. Damn! Trust me; he was fucking clever. I don't know but my competition he was.

'Alok, I want us to…' I was interrupted in between.

'He called us' Alok said.

'Whom are you talking about?' I asked, snootily.

'The Boss' *My ass, I thought.*

'I really don't know it seems to be quite unique. One man, I don't know, came and gave a letter to our constable. And that lazy ass, did not mind to ask him who is he?' Ali said, looking at us. We were at police station of Jaipur. Ali was the head here. There was nothing much one could conclude about him. He had a very bad habit of abusing everyone, inferior to him. For now, he had got the letter.

'What's written in it?' Alok asked.

'You both take a look.' Ali said and passed an A4 size paper towards us which had written text in black ink.

Hello my friends,

Lesser you know me, the more I know you! To know me, you need to find me. Don't worry, I know you. Very well. That is why, I'm giving you the news of someone's death…It's going to happen, very soon.

Friends; I am going to kill everyone, I know.

Your dearest friend Rakesh

'What? This man is announcing his sins. He has also mentioned his name, Rakesh.' Alok said, furiously. I was still wondering why this person is informing the police before committing a crime. Someone may have played prank.

'This can also be a mischievous act.' I said giving the letter to Ali.

'Do you think a prankster did this?'

'I don't think so. It looks like someone is really interested in killing someone. He wants to take revenge, I suggest.' This time it was Alok. Ali was sweating.

'I don't know. Maybe. I think he wants to show us that he is clever than us and police.' I said.

'He is not; I am sure because my constable knows how he looks like. So his sketch is going to help me, to throw him behind the bars. I guarantee you.' Ali said with confidence.

'Ali use your brain, man. If he is going to kill someone, why will he come here? He must have sent someone. To catch him, we need to find that man first. Anyways, we can't blame anyone until the crime has been committed.' I said in a loud voice. I looked at Alok. He looked worried.

'What can I do?' Ali asked.

'Wait and watch.' I said and moved out.

We both stepped out of the Police station. Alok still looked serious like he was calculating something. We stopped at the tea stall.

'Where are you brother? You seem to be uncomfortable.' I said, passing him a glass of tea.

'I was just thinking—I think' He coughed twice.

'Imagine this letter is not a prank. It is just a letter of a man who is trying to show us that he is smarter than us. Why an ordinary man will try to prove he is clever than us?' Alok said was right. At some point, I also thought the same.

'This letter is written by an insane person.' I declared.

'You're right. I do understand many peoples criminal mind. What about a madman? He himself doesn't know what is he going to do? How will we know his next step?'

'That is what I am scared of. I just don't want him to start killing people.'

'What if he starts killing people?'

'He won't stop then.' I said and started biting my nails. I had a bad habit of biting my nails.

I was feeling drowsy while having dinner. At night, I did my work on my own. My main worry was—*the letter.* Who must have sent it? Is he really a madman?

"No….. Stop thinking about it" tired part of me said, loudly to me. I was thinking about this letter a lot. If he is a madman, I am sure he won't take much time to execute his plans. Whom will he kill? I suppose, it is not a prank. He is really a madman. Oh! I am still thinking about it.

I never mind if I did not sleep all night. But, for a reason like this, I don't think so I should be awake.

Someone knocked at my door. I wasn't afraid of opening the door. I knew who had come! Alok was standing in front of me.

'It has happened!' He said.

'What?'

'The murder'

'When and how?'

'Stop asking questions. Let's go.' Alok said.

'It happened just 2 hours ago, behind the Jaipur station. An old man is found murdered brutally. Ali said the murderer has killed him with a hammer. Every part of his body is found injured.' Alok continued.

'Oh! It looks like he wanted to take revenge.'

'I think the same.' Alok said.

'Who first saw the corpse?' I asked.

'A commoner'

'Let's do this my friend.' I said to Alok.

He did not look at me. He was horrified.

Detective Vikrant Gupta's Narrative—II

I and Alok reached the scene of crime at 1.30am. There was lot of common people who already had circled around the dead body to see it once. I was desperate to see the way the murderer had killed the old man. We saw Ali and went to meet him. He had a piece of paper in his hand.

'Ali' I called out for him.

'Vikrant, I want to talk to you both. Let's go to the police station.' Ali said in a low voice and we moved from the site. This was the first time; I had left the crime scene so early. Alok was too feeling weird.

After reaching the police station, Ali showed us that piece of paper. Alok read it for me.

Hello my dear friends,

I will be gone before you come and find this letter. Don't try to find me. It will only show me your stupidity.

This letter is for 12ᵗʰ August. I will be gifting you a dead body.

Stop me, if you can.

Your loving friend Ravi

'This is horrible.' Alok cried. Ali told us that he got this letter from the pocket of the victim.

'He has changed the name. I think he is not a sane person. Our guess was right. He is really a madman. The names he is mentioning are all false.' Alok was silently listening to us.

'This is not what I thought of! How are we going to catch him? He can be anyone.' Ali said loudly.

'I know it is a bit of frustrating. Yes! You're right. He can be anyone. Maybe, he was in the crowd. Maybe, he knows us. One of our friends who has just realized he is not normal.' I said.

'Who is that old man?'

'We found out the old stays in an apartment near railway station with his family. His name is Harish Chandra. He works as a manager at Hotel Royal Residency. He is an old man, why anyone will kill him?'

'That's what we have to find out. We need to pay a visit to his home and his workplace. Now we're going to hospital' I said and got up to leave for the hospital. Alok did not get up.

'Are you not coming with me?'

'No!' Alok replied. 'I don't have the courage to take a look at it.'

'Trust me Vikrant; he has been killed very brutally.' Ali said.

It was a brutal murder, I thought.

After observing Harish Chandra's dead body, all the food I had consumed came out, automatically. I had never seen a dead body of a man who had been killed so badly. In detail, I could say, his face was attacked again and again by a hammer. His legs were blood-stained with many cuts and deadly blows by the same hammer. Harish Chandra's dead body was fully soaked with blood. Why anyone would murder so cruelly? Was it done on purpose?

'It is an inhuman act.' I said as I entered the Ali's office.

'I have something to say.' Alok said in middle of our serious conversation with Ali.

'Go on.'

'I think the murderer was uttermost angry and irritated. The manner he had murdered Harish, I don't think he is happy with his life. Why anybody would commit a crime?' Alok asked.

'For his own pleasure or benefit'

'Absolutely correct. Harish Chandra was not at all a millionaire, he was an ordinary man. So, it is clear this murder is not done with an intention to obtain wealth. There are only two other possibilities now. First possibility, is the murder is done as a revenge and I second possibility is the one we are all afraid of and that is our murderer is an insane person.' Alok stated.

'I spoke to his wife; she says she is not in a proper frame of mind to talk with anyone, right now. I insisted her.' Ali shook his head.

'We have less time. Only three days for 12th August to come.' I said.

'I am sorry but a couple of times she banged the door in front of my face.'

'Let's go and take a look. Ali you stay here. She may bang the door again after looking at your face.' Ali was not so happy to hear it from me. He made a disgusting face and went inside his office. I and Alok had a big job to be done.

HARISH CHANDRA'S HOUSE

'Thank you Mrs. Chandra, I hope you are okay?' I said and sat on a chair which made irksome noise. *Definitely, he's not a rich man.* Harish Chandra's wife Dhanvi Chandra did not bang the door on our face nor did she ask any questions regarding why we were here for. I saw a girl playing with her pocket handkerchief. She was their only daughter.

'Earlier, why you did not entertain police officer Ali when he had come for investigation?' Alok asked.

'I don't trust police officers. They can't do anything. You both have solved many such cases and I know like every time this also you both will hit the bull's eye. I trust you.' Mrs. Chandra said. I felt good and bad at the same time. Good feeling was she trusted me and Alok. Bad feeling was she did not trust police. Well, every Indian thinks the same way. They trust outsiders but not their own people.

'Do you think your husband had any enemies?' I asked, first. Alok looked at me.

'He was a very humble and down to earth man. I have never seen anyone arguing with him. Even at his work place, he behaved nicely with everyone.'

'Are you sure? I am sorry to ask but did you look at your husband's dead body?'

'Of course not' She said and added. 'My brother went to check there and he told me, it is a *blood-curdling* murder. I don't have a strong heart to discern the fact that my husband has been killed mercilessly.'

Her eyes had tears. It conveyed the pain she had within her, at that particular moment.

'We feel terrible too. Have your husband mentioned about any letter he got from a random man?' Alok asked. There was not much she knew about her husband's life outside home.

'He never mentioned. Why Harish would get letters from a random people?' She asked us.

'Sorry, as for now, we can't answer your questions.' I said. Ali told us not to disclose about letters to anyone, not even victim's family members.

'That is fine. She doesn't even know her father is no more.' Mrs. Chandra said pointing towards her daughter. It was an emotional moment.

'What's her name?' Alok grilled.

'Her name is Divya. She is just 9 years old.' She was too young to understand such huge problems.

'She looks a jolly girl. Don't let her know for a while. Allow her to enjoy her childhood.' Alok opined.

Mrs. Chandra smiled at us. We could not say much to her after all she had lost her husband. After asking few more questions, we left from her house.

'What you think?' I asked as we moved out of apartment building.

'No enemies. No trust. I'm confused, man.' Alok answered me. This man must have observed something strange. I better know it soon.

'I don't hear it from you Alok. Something strange you observed? C'mon spill.' I smiled.

'She was hiding something. How come Mrs. Chandra doesn't know anything about Harish's workplace? I found it uncanny.'

'Alok! There are many husbands on this earth who think it's not worthy enough to reveal information about workplace to their wives. Remember, you too don't share our talks with your wife.'

'Our work demands privacy. Did his work demanded privacy?' I know he is more than intelligent.

'This makes you special my friend. Only his workplace can solve this case.' I declared.

'No Vikrant, I don't think so. We can get some news about Harish's work. Perhaps, we can conclude a point.'

'Don't be pessimistic. Be positive.' I said as we marched towards Harish Chandra's workplace.

Hotel Royal Residency: Harish Chandra's Workplace.

Royal Residency hotel was one of the filthiest places I ever visited. Hotel workers wore shabby uniforms, floor was mucky and a fat manager, made me enough furious. Alok was fuming over the place too. Nobody gave us attention plus little did we know. Hotel was working, well. The only thing that grabbed my attention was; many men were visible at sight.

'Are you in charge?' I said as I approached the fat manager. Shit! He was eating samosa. I was also hungry.

'Yes! I am' Fatso answered.

'We want to talk you about Harish Chandra. He was a manager here…'

'And a good friend of mine', fatso interrupted me and said. He left the half-eaten samosa on the counter and directed us towards the waiting room. He told us, his name is Amit. After Harish's death the owner of the hotel appointed him as the manager. He had a big moustache.

'It seems like this hotel is quite famous thoughits condition is suboptimal.' I sassed. He looked at me as if he would deliver a punch anytime soon.

'I know. But the rooms are quite spacious and well ventilated. For your knowledge, this hotel is famous.' Rude response was obvious.

'Well, coming to the point. What kind of a person Harish was?' I said directly coming to the point.

'Harish was a simple man. He was meek and submissive too. Why anyone would kill such a good man? He had no enemies and he only had quality friends.' Amit said. I understood the quality of his friends who eat samosas all day.

"Why am I being so judgemental?" I scolded myself. Wait! Did I ask anything about his enemies?

'Why Harish went home, that night?' Alok enquired.

'Harish always had day shift. He never worked during night.'

'What time he left from here?'

'He usually leaves at 8.30pm.' Amit answered. Amit confidently answered our questions. No sweat. No anger.

'Did anyone ever fought with him? Someone called Rakesh?' I asked.

'Never heard of any such fights' He added. 'Sir, he always helped others. There could be some rare case of him fighting with others. I don't remember any such case.'

'Did he ever say something about letters he got or wrote?'

'No.'

'How were his relations with his wife?' Alok asked.

'Very bad. She never cared for him. She never loved him. Dhanvi only cursed him. Sometimes for him low salary, sometimes for smoking and there were millions of pointless reasons she argued about. Harish used to cry in front of me. He was a hapless human being when it came to marriage.' Amit sobbed.

'We met his wife. She happened to be a good and respectable woman.' I said. *She really looked troubled after her husband's death.*

'Drama is all she can do! That's what Harish always said, she's selfish and dramatic.'

'Do you really think Harish had no enemies?' Alok asked again.

'Except his wife, none I know.' Amit agreed with the fact—Harish had enemies.

We moved out of the hotel, unannounced.

'He is lying. Harish was not a trustworthy person.' Alok said as we waited for the bus to come.

'Let it be at one side. Amit told us, Harish had no enemies. I didn't even ask him about it. Look he was hiding something from us.' I was excited.

'What about Mrs. Chandra not loving Harish or we can say his only enemy?' Alok uttered.

'I'm confused.'

'Harish had one enemy at least.'

'So, you believe Amit?' I said patting his shoulders.

'We can't believe anyone.' Alok said as we got into the bus.

We both had unhappy and strained faces.

DETECTIVE VIKRANT GUPTA'S NARRATIVE—III

When you stay alone in a house, surrounded by boring books and old furniture—you're not blessed. A part of me always wanted a person I could spend my whole life with. Once I also had a dream of having a small and happy family. Life is not that simple. As I found my passion, my dream of having a happy family took a backseat in my life. Priorities change with time. Although I enjoyed investigating work and my life as a detective but still I knew, I could never achieve my dream. Alok had a happy family with whom he could spend time with and make memories for life. *I had no one.*

Next morning, Alok and I got a call from the police station. The constable said that we were called by Officer Ali. Keeping a stone on my heart I took a full day leave from the bank.

'Why have you called us?' I said sonorously.

'Sit down, guys. I have some news.' He said and continued, 'This Harish Chandra was a third-rated man. Harish never cared for his wife. He always fought with everyone and was a very abusive man. Hotel Royal Residency conducts an illegal business of supplying women. This hotel is the spot for enjoyment for all males. Harish also had a wicked business of supplying school girls to wealthy businessmen. You see how many lives he must have ruined. Harish was really a black-hearted man. No wonder someone murdered him.'

Ali talked non-stop for 3 minutes. Mr. Sanjay Jaiswal entered the room with a smile on his face. *Why the hell was he smiling? We are discussing a serious case here.* Sanjay Jaiswal was Ali's boss. He was an arrogant man. He did not have a clean reputation but he did have a brain. I don't know why but I always felt he is not a right man. I and Alok kept a good distance from him. Hey wait? Practically, we both were his rivals.

'Good morning, sir.' We formally greeted him.

'What about the nutcase?' *Is he really interested?*

'We are trying our best sir. He has left no clues. He only left this letter.' Mr Jaiswal read the letter and then kept it on the table. After keeping it, he acted like he was thinking something. Later he said: 'I believe you both will solve this case. Do you really think he is not a sane person?'

I looked towards Alok. Alok looked towards me. In simple words, we were peering at each other's face. We had no answer to his question.

'Don't worry you will get one. Take care.' Sanjay Jaiswal said and left the room.

"Can he read minds?" I thought.

'During the investigation, the fat hotel manager Amit told us: Harish was a humble man.' I added. 'Actually Amit also told us his wife harassed him.' Ali looked horrified. He started sweating. Even Harish's wife did not tell us about Harish evil acts. Now, I was more confused.

'I'm totally confused about this. Who gave you this information?' Alok asked doubting the facts Ali provided.

'My spy' Ali said immediately. He looked annoyed.

'Why everyone is lying? Amit lied because he wanted to hide the evil work his hotel done. I know understand why Mrs. Chandra lying to us?' Alok said louder than usual.

'Maybe it came as a shock to her.' I was narked by Ali's direct answers.

'Was he involved in kidnapping?' Ali shook his head. Suddenly, Alok got up to leave.

'Where are you going?'

'Home'

'What about the case?' I asked.

'What about it? We don't know the suspect. Who is he? How he looks like? We only know he has a damaged mind-set. We lack evidence too. No one is providing us proper information. Damn! Harish's own wife is lying! We cannot go forward with misleading information and evidences. This case is unceasing. It will never end and people will only give us false information.' Alok explained.

'What should we do?' Ali asked.

'Let him commit the next crime.' Alok said and blinked.

We both moved out of the police station. I was shocked by Alok's sudden change of attitude. He never gave up on any case no matter what the cost.

'What was that?' I asked him as we moved into hotel. We both were starving.

'What I said was right! Little we know about our mad friend.'

'We can't just rest doing nothing. We'll have to do something.' I coaxed. Alok laughed. 'Am I joking?'

'No, Vikrant! You're not joking. You know what our madman wants to prove?'

'He wants to prove, he is smarter than us.' I blurted.

'He also wants our attention. He wants his dominance over everyone. He wants to show us that he is powerful than us and others. Let us assume our madman thinks this way. What if we don't give attention to our madman?' Alok said brilliantly and with that my Idlis and his Dosa came on table with delicious aroma. *It looks delicious.*

'Our insane killer will get hyperactive and will try to seek our attention.' Is it making sense? He has already told us that he is going to gift us a dead body. I mean, he is definitely going to kill someone.

'Vikrant' Alok called out for me.

'Yes?' I responded.

'What are you thinking?'

'Alok, our madman knows what he is going to do. He plans the murder before doing it.' I said and added, 'He knows who he is going to kill. Why he is going to kill that particular person. There must be some purpose behind it. We need to know the—purpose.' I whispered.

'How can you say so bluntly?' Alok asked me.

'I suppose, killer knew why he wanted to kill Harish?'

'I can't say anything for now. He doesn't have any purpose, I think so. He is loony and not in his senses. Wait! I have got some information. Antisocial personality disorder, have you heard about it?' Alok said those three extremely confusing words.

'Just now' I smiled.

'ASPD is a personality disorder which most of serial killers suffer from.' Alok gave me some important but not very exciting information about this personality disorder. 'It is also one the hardest disorders to treat.'

Whole Jaipur was now in danger… Everyone needs to be alert and vigilant.

My head was paining. I made black tea for myself and sat on my old rocking chair. I closed my eyes and tried to feel comfortable. I tried to think of nothing— but my very multi-talented mind never slept. I was again forced to think about the killer who was reason behind my headache. *There must be some catch.* Many questions came in my mind:

Why is our killer sending letters to police before committing a crime? Why he wants to prove that he is better than us or police department? No! He has not mentioned my or Alok's name in any letter. Why Harish was killed? What is Harish's past? Why everyone is lying? Fuck! Why am I thinking so much?

Let's wait for 12th August. That's all I can do.

Just when I was going to sleep I remembered: I was free for the evening. I quickly got up and without washing my face I walked out of my house. I hired a rickshaw and told him the destination I wanted to visit. Some tiny bumps in roads made my journey comfortable. I haven't said that I had a good journey. I was standing in front of Hotel Royal Residency. I again met fat manager Amit. Today, he was eating pancakes. *Bloody fatso, I thought.*

'I want to book one room' I said and gave my details to him. I also gave him room charges.

Room was well-maintained. I reminded myself: "I'm here to get information about this hotel".

I stepped outside of my room and started walking in corridors. There was pin drop silence. I moved around every floor but I did not get anything. I came back in my room. I looked myself in mirror; I looked like a defeated warrior. I have spent for living here. Then someone knocked my door. It was a waiter who had brought me a glass of water. 'Thank you!' I said and closed the door.

I cursed myself for coming here. I went everywhere. I even went in the kitchen of the hotel which was not at all clean. I did not get any crucial information. I came here to see hotel's illegal activities but I got nothing. I regret coming here, I said to myself as I passed hotel main gate.

Suddenly I moved back. I re-entered the hotel and went towards the managers' desk. Amit was writing something. He looked up.

'Was Harish a good person?' I asked Amit. Black in his eyes moved downwards.

What Ali said was right.

DETECTIVE VIKRANT
GUPTA'S NARRATIVE—IV

On 12th August, I did not eat or drink anything in morning. Actually I did not sleep at night. Even though, I tried to. I was just waiting near my telephone. Alok called me two times, if I got a call from Ali. I did not get any calls all day. I called Alok over my place for dinner. He agreed without hesitation. I remember, exactly at 9.30pm I got a call from the police station. The officertold me, the murder has happened. He told me to reach near Jalebi Chowk (near the city palace).

Another murder had happened. These crimes should be stopped as soon as possible. We can't afford to lose more lives. This has to stop.

'These crimes must no go on. We need to find the murderer very soon.' I said as we walked together.

'Very soon' Alok said.

After thirty minutes, we were at the crime scene. There were very less police officers who had come for investigation. This time victim was a woman. She was in her mid-twenties, had long hair which had blood and she was also attacked by a hammer. Her face was terribly injured. One could hardly recognize her. *This must be done to hide her identity.* Alok, I and Ali rushed to our office (Alok's second home). Alok and I always kept our confidential and case related documents in our office. It was Alok's second home.

'I'm coming here for the first time.' Ali said as he moved inside. Alok had built it 5 years ago. Alok had a habit of penning down the investigative stories which we solved together. Very rarely he came to write and whenever he came he called me to accompany him. We both had keys of this house. I saw Alok in the kitchen making black tea for both of us. Ali removed a piece of paper and kept it on the table. I immediately got to know, it was the murderer's letter for us. It was different from previous two letters. I read it in clear voice:

> *Hello my friends,*
>
> *I'm very close to you. Still this girl went up with ease... Detective Rajput and Gupta, both are helpless. If you try to find me, you won't get me ever. Are you trying or given up? Not so soon.*
>
> *Mark the next date: 15 August. Independence Day!*

Please catch me. HAHAHA!

Yours loving and caring friend, Kumar

'Oh My God, is this fiend going to commit another crime? This is more frightening than any other case, Vikrant.' Alok said, acting peculiarly. He has mentioned my and Alok's name. That means he knows us. He has given us a very clear message, he someone we know, closely. This hint can be useful.

'I know, Alok. It is very painful to watch so many people die. My soul is burning…' Ali winced.

'He is someone who I and Alok closely know and understand. He can be one of our friends. The murderer has clearly revealed it. He has written; *if you try to find me, you won't get me ever.* This is understandable. We find the one whom we don't know. Our half job is done. We only need to find the one who has been killing people, wickedly.' I said confidently. Alok and Ali both looked at me as if I was a genius.

'This can also be written to distract us. Anyways, to reach there we need to know about the victim first. This time he has killed a girl with equal anger and insanity.' Ali said, rapidly. Even I have seen the body, I wanted to say but I did not. Alok was quietly sipping his black tea.

'We cannot know anything about victim until morning.' I gasped. Ali waved us goodbye. He had to meet doctors so he went. Alok looked quite disturbed. So was I.

'Alok, I know you want this to end very soon. I hope it ends, early. We can't let more people die.' I said holding his hand. Tears started flowing from his eyes. Damn! He was crying like a five year old baby. I had never seen this part of him. *He feels guilty if he is not able to find a murderer, I realized.*

'Vikrant, I can't let other people die because of my or your smartness. Whoever the killer maybe, I don't care. He only wants to show us his cleverness and I think he is smarter than us.' Alok was saying loudly.

'Alok, why are you giving up on this case?' I too shouted this time.

'As I said earlier, I don't want people to die because of us.'

'Who said he will stop killing people if we publicly accept that we are dumb and he is intelligent? Did he mention this in any of his letters? I know this case is harder than previous cases.' I admitted.

'Okay. Let us acknowledge a truth: our murderer is a genius. He never leaves any evidence. He is properly kills people only to show us he is cleverer than us. Look, ultimately, he wants to create a kind of his terror among people. For example: if we stop investigation on this case and he continues with his evil acts. So, can you say who won the battle between us?' I asked Alok.

'The murderer'

'Exactly my point. The murderer is madly murdering not only to show us his clever mind but he also wants to create fear in people's mind. It is not our fault so please stop feeling guilty. All we need to do is catch him and win the battle.' I said motivating him. I could see Alok's sparkling eyes. I was scared if he would cry again. But he did not. In fact, he smiled. I was happy to see Alok Rajput back.

We all have ups-downs. All we need is that one person who holds us during our tough times and never lets us fall down and truly speaking the same person puts us up where we deserve to be. That night, I cried too. We both slept in our office (Alok's second home).

Next morning, newspapers had articles and stories related to our unsuccessful investigation. Though in India, there were few detectives but we had a reputation. Good reputation, I'd say. It was a kind of humiliation for us. Alok looked slightly more disconcerted than me. Indian Express left us red-faced by mentioning we had no suspects after the second murder. They also had a point. We wanted to point someone but we had no one to doubt. I and Alok took five days leave from our respective banks. We cannot let the third murder happen, I said to myself. I took a reluctant bath. We both skipped our breakfast not because we were not hungry, we had nothing to eat. We stepped out of the house in search of breakfast. We satisfied ourselves with tea and *Upma*. We reached police station by 8am.

We directly moved to Ali's cabin. He was busy scanning something. He looked exhausted. He would've worked whole night. 'Hey, what are you leering at?'

'Good to see you both. You read this.' He said and tossed a copy of Indian Express towards us. I nodded.

'The victim's name is—Akanksha Bhatt. She was a student here. She was doing BA from Maharani Girls College. She was missing from yesterday morning. She did not even attend her college yesterday. Akanksha was not seen by any of her college friends too. I think she was kidnapped in the morning from the girl hostel. Why our madman was after her?' Ali said, rapidly.

'We will definitely talk about it, later. I want to reread all the three letters and the reports written by your department.' Alok said in a firm voice.

'My department is a useless one. I wrote the reports for this case.' He said and hunted for the files. He handed the files in my hand. 'Why you need them?'

'Just for personal check, my brother'

'You interrogated her friends. What about Akanksha's parents?' I asked.

'She is an orphan. She was picked by a charitable trust when she was just 5 years old. Later, she turned out to be a smart girl and rest is history. Akanksha's friends knew a little about her.' Ali explained. Very silent victim this time, my mind forced me to think about this.

'Why our madman killed her?' Alok questioned. An unanswerable question for now, I answered to myself.

'He is mad. He can do anything. No one knows who is he? There is no purpose behind it.' Ali said coughing out more. He smoked a lot.

'No, Ali you're completely mistaken. He has a purpose. Some purpose.Some mysterious purpose.' I spoke.

'Yesterday, we also concluded that he is one of our friends or relatives.' This time it was Alok.

'I really don't know. I can't say. We don't have any such proof against anyone.'

'Are you declaring we won't get him ever?' I said in a loud and clear voice.

'Did I say that?' I was worried about everything.

'What should be our next move?' Alok asked Ali.

'I have something to say.' I interrupted before Ali could speak. He nodded as a go on sign.

'We know the same person has murdered both victims. No doubt about it. So all I have to say is—no crime is perfect. He must have done some mistake.'

'We have got no evidence from the crime scene.' Ali interrupted me. I made one of those teacher-angry-on-student faces.

'I am not talking about evidences. There must be something common in both the crimes. I have seen one common thing in both the crimes. The murderer has murdered both of them in dark. Even though Akanksha was missing the whole day but our killer killed her few hours before throwing her on the road. How he finds it so easier to dump a dead body on a road? There must be someone who had seen him dumping the corpse. I don't think he has a partner. If we are going in a right direction then we need to find out two things promptly: first that one common thing and second who he is going to kill next.' I ended my short talk. My both friends look down towards the floor.

'So Mr. Vikrant Gupta, how're we going to find that one common thing or the next person who is going to be killed?' Alok said with his voice filled with sarcasm.

'To my logic, there must be a vehicle or he must have used a car to transport Akanksha's dead body from the place he had killed her to the place we found her. Maharani Girls College is just 12 km away from the city palace. We need to find the vehicles went towards that area from a particular period of time till a particular time limit. Trust me; not much drivers drove their vehicle towards the city palace during night time.' I said.

'You mean to say that we should go near the city palace and question people if they have seen Akanksha in the car.

It will take a whole bloody day.' Alok cried. I looked at Ali. For the next two or three hours, police will be very busy. 'Is it yours?' Alok asked Ali pointing towards a book kept on the table. Great Expectations by Charles Dickens, I read the cover page.

'Yes!'

'Can I borrow it from you?' Alok requested.

'Yes! Return it on time. I hate sharing Dickens novels' Ali said and gave us a glossy smile. I did not smile back.

'Why you read such novels?' I asked wanting to know more.

'Why you don't read?' *Nice answer, I thought.*

I was disappointed, displeased and dissatisfied after the search result. Jaipur Police did not gain anything in four hours of search. Not a single person saw her near City Palace with the murderer. How's it possible? Does he have any supernatural powers? Is he a magician?

Well, there was one flaw in Akanksha.

Akanksha was engaged with a business of supplying girls to businessmen and whoever paid more.

I was shocked to hear it, initially. But, Ali cleared everything to us. There were girls in hostel who needed more money to live in Jaipur because their families had little to earn and spent. So, Akanksha was the head.

'I understand his pattern, Ali. He is killing people who are doing illegal businesses around the city. I think he is acting like some psycho serial killer who has come in action to clean the society and save it from harmful activities.' Alok said. *He can be right.*

'I already told you both, he has some purpose. Our murderer is on a mission to save common people from evil occurrences happening in our city. There's still one question left: why is he leaving letters for us? Specifying our names?'

'He is gone mad, Vikrant. He must be thinking—we all are useless so teach us a lesson. We are popular so he is teasing us. I only know, what he is doing is not at all correct. He is on a wrong track.'

'He is really insane.' Ali murmured.

'We at least know something about him.' Alok looked happy.

'He knows us!' I said to myself.

DETECTIVE VIKRANT GUPTA'S NARRATIVE—V

It was heavily raining outside when I completed reading those three letters, for the fifth time. I was trying to understand his mentality. I wasn't able to. I and Alok had discussed about the murder over 100 times by now. We were almost empty handed. We only had three letters written by three different men (which we thought was written by one man). No evidence, no suspects and nothing solid against anyone. We were fooled by someone. Someone who was better than us. 'You look lost?' Alok said.

'I am really lost.' I said making a face to divert his mind. He was also upset but he did not let his face define it.

'I know. Any updates from Ali?'

'He is trying is best. He is informing everyone in the city and specially lawbreakers. They are the targets.'

'He should put them behind the bars.'

'He won't'

'Why? Shouldn't he?' Alok asked. I wanted to put his face into mud and press it hard against it. He knew politics and their games still he demanded an answer from me.

'I am not answerable to you.'

Alok kept quiet for some time and again asked, 'Do we know him? I mean the murderer.'

'I think so. This is a kind of revenge he is barging on us. He wants us to suffer.' I said and added, 'I know in these years we have made many enemies but why is he hurting others? He should directly kill us. The most important part is security of local people. No one has the right to kill anyone. This is confusing me. What he wants to prove rests with him.'

'Last night we discussed about it. He is not a sane person. He is killing wrongdoers.'

'I don't understand why is he killing them if he is insane?'

'Vikrant, there are some people who love their motherland, unconditionally and madly, of course. He cannot stand bad things happening in our society.' Alok said. *I just don't understand.*

'He knows everything about the person he is going to kill, I am saying this because there is not a single proof we have derived from the crime scene. He is just so perfect.' I had a point. Planned murder is what we call it.

'This is possible. He can pull out information about a person before attacking him. Once he is ready, he attacks.'

'If he is planning murders than he is definitely not an insane man.'

'You can be both at the same time. Mad plus a planner to keep going. After all, he doesn't want us to arrest him.' Alok too had a point but I found it senseless.

'If he is what you're talking about then particularly he will be the most alluring man I will ever meet.'

'This crime is a baffling mystery, Vikrant.' Alok said when he saw me getting up. He wanted to talk more about it. *It would be waste of time, I thought.*

'Our murderer is more puzzled man.' I said.

At last, there is someone who I am unable to understand.

The wall clock showed me the time—11.45pm.

Alok and I looked at each other. After fifteen minutes, anything can happen. Who is going to be the victim this time? I thought. Where is Ali in all this? I haven't talked to him since morning. Morning, he called to inform us, everything was going on fine.

Meanwhile, Independence Day, had come. We were awake all night. We did not receive a single call form anyone. There was a sense of happiness but disappointment struck soon. Head Mistress of a highly reputed school was found dead on the terrace of her school, at 10.30am. The school was in Tillawala, Jaipur.

At the crime scene, we were welcomed by bunch of news reporters. This humiliation, I cannot handle, I thought. Alok and I met Ali. He appeared to be upset with whatever had happened. We told the police officers to take reporters in an empty classroom. I was not happy with so much of noise, attention and the questions reporters were continuously babbling. As they left, Ali started:

'The name of the Head Mistress was Miss Ambika Parmar and her age was 48. Like every time, this crime was also done by hammer. She was murdered 10 hours before. Ambika resides near Jaipur station with her brother. There is not much I could say. He did not leave any clues.' Ali said, while he was noting some points. He was not particularly giving us the needed attention. I was feeling, if we're not important then please let us go. Ali never ignored us.

'Anything else' I asked.

'Vikrant, I don't want to talk anything right now. First let us, go and attend the press otherwise they would abuse us for disregarding them.' Ali said, clearly and moved away. *Fuck you; I abused him in my mind.*

Interacting With Press

There was an electric atmosphere in the classroom as we entered some of the reporters got up and some did not even care to see. They were busy in their own world. Generally, press meetings don't happen in a classroom. In India, after three brutal murders, by a same person, our press gets furious and question wherever they want. I was tensed with this idea of interacting with reporter because even after three murders we were at zero. I tried to focus. Alok looked confident. With my eyes I asked him:

'What's going on?'

'Let this go'

Ali came in and opened the case file and kept it on the table for reference. The class was almost full by 20 reporters sitting individually, each on one bench. Though, people were from the same channel, they tried to utilize the whole area. Ali provided them the needed information and also revealed photocopies of all the three letters. Photographers stepped forwards and took photos of the evidence. With every passing minute, I was feeling more and more nervous. Alok looked relaxed. *How can he be relaxed?*

I and Alok had some discussions with Ali about how much information we should provide public through press for now. We almost had more of our psychological theories than any actual or real evidence, excluding the letters. We decided to disclose everything we had discussed.

'I know. We all are here for good. I would like to take one question at a time. Mr Rajput and Mr Gupta would freely answer you. So, you all can start.' Sanjay Jaiswal said. He was sitting in the centre.

'This case is one of the hardest ones. We admit it. I would like to ask you Mr Ali where the investigation has reached? And are you still with no suspects?' A woman from the second bench said.

'As for now, the investigation is going on, still. According to us, the man who is killing people is mentally ill. He may be having some mental disorder. The man only provides us the dates, when is he going to commit his crime. With every murder, we are investigating about how he does it so easily without leaving evidence? How he looks like? How he thinks like? When we think like a madman, it is hard to predict his next crime. We don't have a suspect. The backgrounds of both victims are not strong. Harish (first victim) supplied girls to businessmen. Akanksha (second victim) was a student but was also a prostitute or a call girl we can say. We can't say anything about Ambika Parmar because the investigation will take time. So, you can observe that Harish and Akanksha can have many enemies. We cannot blame anyone until we find some solid proof.' Ali said.

'Next question is for Mr. Vikrant. What the murderer is trying to prove by killing people?'

'Well, it is difficult to say. The murderer is openly challenging me and Alok. We both had a joint discussion about this. We concluded a point. The point is: The murderer wants to show he is clever than us. I suppose, he is jealous of us or he is really mad.

Another concept attached to this case is: the person is only killing people who are carrying on unlawful business and people who are harmful to the society in some ways. There is some purpose behind his every crime.' I said, excited. Before the next question, Sanjay Jaiswal said loudly:

'If he has a motive behind his crimes then I'm sure he is a sane person.' I sniggered. *Maybe he is right!*

'What can be the purpose behind these crimes? Can you explain Mr. Vikrant?'

'You people ask questions which a person cannot answer.' I smiled. Sanjay lookedunhappy.

'What are evidences except the three letters?' Someone asked Ali. He looked at me.

'We have not got any evidence from the scene of the crime.' People who were present started jabbering. Ali told something very exciting to them. *They are going to freak now.*

'So, you mean, investigation has been carried out carelessly?'

'No. We have been responsible and attentive. We have considered each and every fact. Blaming us is not a solution. Solution is to cooperate with us. Throughout the case, we have tried to solve the case. But I don't know who is he? What kind of criminal is he? He is too smart. He has done every crime, smoothly.' Sanjay retorted. 'I know this crime is arduous but not unsolvable.'

Sanjay Jaiswal may have a bad reputation but he helped when it came to serial killings or hard-to-understand-crimes. Ali and his team were trying. We were seeing their hard work. But only one fact was annoying me, it gave no results. Reporters fired more questions majorly related to police and their work. I was sitting there clueless about the crime. The safety of local people became the major issue. Many reporters asked Ali about safety of common people. To my surprise he responded positively and assured their safety. I closed my eyes trying to feel comfortable. But it was me. I can never be comfortable after three successful brutal crimes. I had seen many criminals but this one was baffling me. It was hard to think about him. So dangerous, using a hammer to kill people. Who is so heartless??

'So, Mr. Vikrant is it mortifying for you and Mr. Alok?' One reporter asked me and Alok. Alok took the initiative to answer.

'What?' Alok laughed. 'Before I answer your question, answer me. Let's take an example, your child has demanded a toy which you cannot bring it for some genuine reason. He gets angry on you. Do you think it is embarrassing?'

'No.'

'Why do you expect us to be mortified? Why should we feel ashamed?' Alok said, smiling.

He was right! But it was humiliating. We both knew it. But we did not want to admit it.

'Last question sir, do you think without evidence will you be able to catch the criminal?'

'It's not always about physical evidence. It is also a mind game. I know evidences are of great importance in a case like this. But sometime you get a hard nut to crack. No crime is perfect. Perfection is harder to execute in crimes. We are trying figure out things. I hope we catch him soon. He must be very happy to get such publicity.' Alok said and smiled.

'Finally, press undressed us!' said Sanjay Jaiswal.

"You deserve to be" I wanted to answer.

DETECTIVE VIKRANT GUPTA'S NARRATIVE—VI

I and Alok sacrificed our lunch. Ali told us, to come with him to police station. I felt like bashing him. Initially, he treated us like dogs now he wants to chat with us. My mind wasn't working properly because I was extremely hungry. I could have eaten petals of a flower. We reached police station after a bumpy ride. Jaipur was not yet developed properly. Ali offered us tea. I agreed and asked the constable to bring biscuits with it. Suddenly, Ali went out of his office. Alok and I sat there looking each other's face. He gave me an understanding nod. Tea came with brown coloured biscuits. I pounced at it like a beggar who had not eaten anything from five days.

'We got nothing, huh?' Sanjay Jaiswal said from behind. Ali was with him. I thought of offering him biscuits but then gave up on it.

'Yeah right' I said, after my not so satisfying lunch. Should I call it lunch?

'I want to meet her brother.' Alok said and stood up.

'I suppose he is coming here' Ali said and stopped us.

'What about the next letter?' Sanjay Jaiswal asked Ali.

'Strange thing is that; I did not get letter for the next crime.'

'What?' I and Alok said in unison. *He did not leave any letter.*

'Do you think this crime is done by any other person?'

'No! I don't think so because the way of killing exactly matches pervious crimes. Ambika has been killed, brutally. I have also got the information regarding her. She was a corrupted woman. She took donations for admissions. After paying the amount, the students were thrown out of the school. Whenever families of innocent students complained about such evil practices to police station, school used their political support. Therefore, Ambika has been killed. The murderer didn't left any letter this time. I think he is planning something big. He doesn't want to disclose his next murder…and' Ali was interrupted by a constable. Constable said:

'We have found a dead body at the rear side.'

'How's this possible?' Ali hollered.

'I don't know' said the constable.

'You guys sleep all day.' This was the fourth murder.

The dead body was identified by police after 3 hours. It was a corpse of a man. His name was Ajit Parmar. He was Ambika's brother. This murder was more interesting for me because he was not killed brutally. There was just a small slid cut on his neck. He must have died slowly. Ajit's mouth was covered by a napkin. Ali checked victim's clothes. He found an A4 size paper from back pocket of his trouser. This was it. The murderer had killed Ambika's brother and hurled his body at the back side of the police station. How can he be so clever? For a moment, I thought this case was unsolvable. Who is he? Who is thinking so much? Murder after murder… However, this murder was dissimilar to others. But the paper made it clear.

'This serial murderer should be stopped, very soon. This is fourth one. What's written on the letter?' Sanjay Jaiswal asked. He must be a fearless soul. He must be so clever. Tossing a dead body on the back side of police station is no joke, right?

'I think Alok and Vikrant should leave the room.' Ali said not showing us the letter.

'Why should we?' I protested.

'I see…I think you will not be happy after reading this. So, I think you should not read it.'

'I want to read it, Ali.' Alok said and snatched the letter from his hand. He read it in his mind. There was abrupt peace. Alok finished reading it. I asked him, about the letter. He shook his head and handed me the letter. I looked at Alok, angrily, and tried to focus on that letter. Well, it was not a letter.

BREAKING NEWS:

Detective Alok Rajput and Detective Vikrant Gupta—DEAD

Date: 22/08/1972

Day: Tuesday

I am not a psycho.

The paper slipped from my hand. Yes! He is not an insane person.

I got a hangover without drinking. All our investigation, discussions and various theories—now had no value. It was all planned by someone. Someone. That someone is so confident. He wants to see us in breaking news. Many thoughts were passing by. I and Alok had lost everything. After some days, we could be killed. How finely he wrote, he is not a psychopath.

'Don't worry. Nothing will happen to you both. We will lock you up for that one day. Let's see how he kills you inside the bars?' Ali gave us an easy path.

'No! I want to meet him.' Alok said standing up. 'I want to know who he is. Why he wants to kills us? If he wanted to kill us then why did he killed others? There must be a strong reason behind it. I want to know that reason.'

'Reason can be…our defamation.' I said.

'You can be right!'

'This letter can also be deception. How can you be so confident about him not being mad? He must be playing some other game with us.' Sanjay Jaiswal argued. Alok was not in a mood to understand things.

'I don't think so. It can't be deceptive. First, he has not mentioned any name. Second, we need to take him seriously. After all, he has murdered four people.'

'How can you be so assertive?'

'Assertive is not the right word. I'm just trying to predict what's heading towards us. And somewhere in my heart I believe this person doesn't lie when he becomes a criminal.' Alok said making a strange face.

'He is already a criminal.' Sanjay Jaiswal would never stop. I was standing there silently hearing their argument.

'I can now tell you the description of the murderer. He is a middle class man. No doubt, the murderer is young and has enough power to hit people, badly. While, everyone is searching for the killer; our murderer enjoys and observes what is happening around. As I said earlier, he is middle class. So, he gets the necessary information. He thinks he is the cleverest. But he is not. I will show him he is not. Why he wants to kill us? This question can be perfectly answered by him only. That's why I want to meet him.' Alok described him in few words. Alok can be right. Perhaps, we had only one option left.

Wait for 22/08/1972.

'I want to investigate Ambika's house. Ajit knew something about that murderer. Otherwise why would he kill him?' I thought after writing a report on Ajit's murder. It was a short report. Medical reports were expected to come at six. My Independence Day, went in police station discussing about crimes. Rain started outside. I looked at it. I played with few raindrops. It reminded me of my childhood. I used to play with my friends during raining season. I missed those days. Those golden days, would never come back in my life. One of the best parts of my childhood was my friends. Medical reports came, interrupting my childhood thoughts and memories. Ali read it and told us:

'Medical says Ajit was killed on the same time when Ambika was killed. This means, the murderer has killed both of them at the same time. But the strange part is that, we got Ajit's body from the rear side. I guess he wants to show us his bravery.' Ali said.

'This only shows how powerful he is. He can kill both of us, together.' Alok said.

'What are you saying?' I literally shouted at him.

'Let's move. Next stop: Ambika's house.' Alok said as if he was a bus conductor.

He stepped out quickly. Ali and I looked at each other.

Ambika's Apartment

'They fought every day. Ambika did wrong thing to Ajit. She never married neither she let him marry. He came home late night fully drunk and fought with her. Many times, we warned them but it was of no use. Sometimes he used to hit her. She lived her life in mess.' Overweighed Sunanda told us. Sunanda was Ambika's neighbour.

'Why she did not marry anyone?' I asked avoiding Ajit's drinking part.

'Some 10 years back, Ambika was seeing someone. He cheated on her. This cheating thing—negatively affected her and she decided not to marry anyone.'

'That time her age must be 38. Why she did not marry, earlier?'

'I don't know. She came here only 12 years back.' Sunanda said.

'Bloody shit! See what I have got.' Ali came hurrying towards me. He had a photo frame in his hand. He showed it to me. It was a frame which had a black and white photograph of Ambika and Mohan.

Unexpected struck me hard.

Mohan Manohar Pandey came to Rajasthan with a simple aim of earning lots of money by unfair means. Mohan during his initial days used to pick pockets and purse. He was petty thief. Mohan's family came to Jaipur searching for him. They found him and told him to come with them but he was in no one's control. He abused his own parents and even smacked his father right across his face. After looking at his behaviour his parents complained to police about his wrongdoings and they did put him behind the bars. "One day, I will take revenge", Mohan said his parents before they left. After passing 10 months in prison, he became more aggressive. When he was in the custody of police, he made wrong contacts. At the age of 25, he decided to choose a wrong path and murdered his own parents. Mohan was listed in most wanted criminals list. So, he left Bihar where his parents stayed and came back to Jaipur. Next 3 months, he lived his life in mess. He did many robberies and harassed many people for money. Then he joined a gangwho kidnapped children for money. That is when I came to know about him. A case was registered and Ali was the investigating officer of the case. Mohan had kidnapped a boy of a very rich Marwari family. Mohan and his group demanded a ransom of one crore. This was large amount and higher authorities were putting pressure on Ali and me. At that time, I did not know Alok. Ali and I investigated for whole 24 hours non-stop, and eventually we found the boy. We got that boy from a warehouse. But Mohan was still missing. He departed before Ali and I arrived. Mohan was smart. He knew he would be checked at every bus station, railway station so he did not try to escape. By using Ali's contacts, we finally located him. We raided that area and caught him. Like every criminal, he offered us bribe. We refused. Mohan was found guilty in the eyes of law and Mohan was sentenced to 10 years of imprisonment. During further interrogation, he was forced to reveal about his earlier life and his previous crimes. However, the day, I met him he told me; he will make me suffer when his time will come. I ignored him. I just walked away and never thought about him.

DETECTIVE VIKRANT GUPTA'S NARRATIVE—VII

I told Alok the whole story related to Mohan Manohar Pandey. Alok got up and drank a full glass of water. He also offered to me. I needed it more than him; I was talking continuously. There was eerie silence for few minutes. Ali too had nothing to say. We were in deep trouble.

'He should still be in jail.' Alok said.

'No. Some local politician using his powers got him out of it. I don't know what connection does Ambika had with him? I think the man she was dating 10 years back was Mohan. You remember, Sunanda saying the man Ambika was dating cheated on her. I guess that man was Mohan because we know him, he is a born devil.' Ali said, applying little amount of logic.

'I think the same but why he killed these people?' I was confused, again. Mohan was not foolish enough to murder such people who were not related to him.

'He wants to spoil your reputation, brother.'

'Why he wrote his name?' I said pointing towards Alok. Alok turned away.

'It's maybe because he now works with you.' Ali had answers to everything.

'Can you give me that letter?' Alok asked.

'We should take a leave.' I said. I was worried about my life. Ali noticed tension that appeared on my face. He came forward and hugged me tight and said:

'I'll make sure nothing happens to you and Alok!' I was about to cry then thought it's crazy to be sentimental at police station. I looked at Alok he was busy reading our death note.

'Don't read it' I said.

'What do you think?' Alok asked me. I was busy in my own thoughts.

'Huh?' I said, stupidly.

'I asked, what do you think about the murderer?'

'I think Mohan can be behind these crimes. But I have not seen him since he is out. I can't say anything right now. Please Alok I don't want to talk about it, right now. Let me get some sleep.' I said out of frustration.

Alok called home. I was upset. I quietly stepped aside. Questions encountered my mind one by one:

Is Mohan the murderer we are searching for? What will he do to us? Will he himself come to us and kill us? Or he can send someone to kill us? Is that politician behind him? Why are we unable to solve this case? No evidences, of course. Who is so clever? Who is he? There must be something we are missing.

'Hey, lost?' Alok said interrupting my chain of thoughts.

'We're missing something very crucial related to our case. It's all mind game, Alok. I say you, Mohan is not mad. He is a planner. Master planner' I said. Actually, what I said was 95% truth. 5% I doubt.

'Mohan Manohar Pandey needs to be found soon.' Alok said as if he was a judge.

'You know people who know him. Where can we find him?'

'It was 7 years back, Alok. Do you want me to remember him for so long?'

'We can find that politician. Ali can tell us.' Alok said and called Ali. Those days, networks died before getting connected. Alok got the line as busy. He tried again and this time he got connected.

'Hello'

'I want to meet that politician friend of Mohan.' Alok said directly. He ended his call soon and told me:

'Ali is calling that politician to police station, tomorrow. That politician is not linked to politics anymore and now working as a social worker. I hope he will be useful to us.'

'I hope so.'

Newspaper took our death note on a new height. They published it. Many newspapers published some unreasonable articles and people loved it. It is always that people like nonsense things and are not agog to know the actually truth behind it. Anyways, we got public support. We received many flowers with some uncommon emotions attached to it. People wrote notes to us. Next day, morning we went to police station. Mr Jitender Sukhadia, the politician who had helped Mohan to rescue from prison was waiting for us. Jitender looked like a simple man. In

India politicians only have simple looks but they are not at all simple. He was not tall nor did he look smart. He had a pencil-thin moustache.

'Hello, he is Alok and I...'

'And you are Vikrant' He knows us. Jitender smiled. I don't like his smile, I said to myself.

'We want to know about Mohan Pandey' Ali asked him. I could see anger on Jitender's face.

'That bastard. He screwed us. I helped him getting out of this jail and he carried on his illegal work at my place. I thought he can work for me but he cannot work for anyone. He is mean. He can only work for himself. He got me arrested for work I never did. He used to hide drugs in my car. He was aware of the fact that no one would check my car and one day I was caught with drugs. I tried to explain but no one was ready to listen to me. When I got out of the jail, no one supported me. I lost all the powers I had. I met Mohan after that and confronted him but he abused me. I never return into politics. Few years back, Mohan murdered a woman for gold and money. I did not pay attention to that news. He is an unpromising man, I tell you. You can't trust him.' Jitender said as if we were hiring Mohan.

'Anything else you know about him?' Alok asked.

'I only know this much.'

'You know her?' I asked showing him Ambika's photograph.

'Ambika Parmar!' Jitender bawled. Ali was shocked to see Jitender's reaction.

'How do you know her?'

'Ambika was Mohan's love. Is she dead?'

'Yes, someone killed her.' Jitender gave us an understanding nod.

'They were together some 10 years back. Whenever Mohan came for a party, she came with him. They were close and Ambika was ready to marry him. Mohan also truly loved her. I don't know how she got to know about Mohan's kidnapping business and she left him. Mohan tried to convince her but it was of no use. She was a teacher.' Jitender explained us the reason behind Ambika's murder. Ambika left him for her good and Mohan made her leave the world for his satisfaction.

'I think this Mohan has planned everything and bounced back dangerously.' I said.

'Is he an emotional person?' Ali asked.

'I told you, he can do anything for his own pleasure or benefits.'

'Answer what I am asking, yes or no?' Ali said in his strict policeman voice.

'No he is not an emotional person. In fact, he became heartless after his break up with Ambika.' I was thinking where he can be.

'Do you need anything else inspector?' Jitender asked and stood up. Ali shook his head. Jitenderleft without uttering a word. I noticed Alok was playing with pencil.

'So?' Ali started.

'I think he is speaking the truth.' I said.

'Why Mohan wants to take his revenge after so many years?' *He wants to kill you too, my brother.*

'What do you mean?'

'I mean... nothing.' Alok stopped and again started playing with pencil. He was behaving weird.

'Do you think we should launch a search operation?' I questioned showing my mental status.

'Are you out of your mind? We only got his photograph with Ambika one of the victim and we can only doubt him because of your history. I'm a bit serious about him because he told you, he will make you suffer. We don't have anything solid proof against him.'

'By the way, Ali, do we have anything solid against anyone?' I said with my voice louder.

'No! We tried Vikrant, you know.' He replied.*Bastard, I thought.*

'Ali you've done nothing in this case! You've become useless!' I yelled at him. Constables and other inspectors were peeping into Ali's room. I had never shouted at him. Alok was dumbstruck.

'Well done Mr. Vikrant Gupta. I remember once in an interview you told, "I live for people. My duty is to protect public and I can die for them." Now you're changing your attitude when it has come to you. Well done, Vikrant. I'm so proud of you.' Ali said in sarcasm and clapped. I looked the other way.

'It is not only about me. It is about everyone. Four murders, we have got nothing. Ali, I don't care about my life. What about others?' I said, calmly.

'Everyone will be safe after 22nd August. I guarantee you. I have a plan.' Ali said.

'What is it?' Alok said.

'Listen, let the murderer be prepared for 22nd. This time we know whom he is going to murder. This time we will be prepared for him.' Ali said and smiled. He told us his plan. I was not confident, yet.

DETECTIVE VIKRANT GUPTA'S NARRATIVE—VIII

Two days passed. Nothing much happened. No murder, so this time the killer was sure about murdering us. With the help of some other sources we got to know Mohan was in Jaipur. Many people knew him but were afraid to disclose information about him. We agreed to Ali's plan. His plan was simple. We should wait and watch. He told us, "Let the murderer come to you." There would be bunch of inspectors outside my house ready and alert to catch the murderer. I doubted his plan because the way he had killed people, I have never seen. When he comes, where he goes, no one knows. Then how the fuck we are going to trap him? I was confused and irritated when someone knocked the door. Alok opened the door. He was not able to see anyone. I got up from the chair and went outside the house. We were at Alok's second home (our office). I looked at around. There was no one…

'Did you see anyone running from here?' I asked. Alok shook his head.

'Who knocked on the door?'

'I don't know. Some kid must be playing, leave it Vikrant.' Alok said as we moved in. I was not happy and a naughty kid is playing with our door. After few minutes someone banged on our door. This time I went running towards it. Again, there was no one. Sadly, I was pulling the door when I saw there was a box kept in front of the door. It was a wooden box. I picked that box and came inside.

'What is this?' Alok said and slightly touching the box. I had a bad feeling about opening that box. I opened it. There was a packet inside it. I unpacked and saw there was blood inside a bottle. There was also a note attached to it. I read it clearly:

Dear friend

This one is for you Mr. Rajput. Let's have some more fun, man.

Yours friend

I was unable to get a word out after reading the note. "Mr Rajput", was the person standing beside me and he was gifted a bottle of blood by someone. Alok looked at the blood and rushed towards the telephone. Within one minute, he came back. He looked worried.

'We have to go, Vikrant.'

'Huh..?'

'My home' He said. I understood the reason behind his worry. During our journey of hardly, 20 minutes I saw another personality popping out of Alok. He was disturbed.

'If I lose my wife or children, I am not going to leave him alive.' Alok promised. We reached his apartment at 2.30. There was silence. We went and rang the doorbell. No one responded. Alok always kept an extra key with him which helped us to get inside the house. As entered we saw blood. Only blood. The floor was fully covered by blood. Someone had killed his wife, ruthlessly. Alok went down on his knees with an emotionless look. I was shocked by this. We didn't even think of something like this. Alok started crying and screaming loudly. Tears welled up in my eyes, too. But, I had to be strong owing to the fact that I had to control Alok. I called Ali with his team which included useless inspectors and constables. Later, after the call, I tried to console Alok. He looked defeated. *While serving for people he lost his wife, forever.* Suddenly, he got up looking here and there.

'Kids should be here, anytime?' Alok choked.

'Don't worry. I will wait outside. As they come, I will leave them to neighbour's house.' I said and got up. I opened the door and saw Ali standing outside. He gave me a sympathy look and went inside.

Alok's kids came at 3.30 and I told his neighbour to look after them. They did not ask any questions because they knew the actual problem. I called out, Alok's neighbourMr Singh.

'I want to ask…' I found it harder to ask him questions regarding the death of my best friend's wife. In the meantime, Alok came and stood beside me.

'Have you heard my wife screaming prior to 12?' Alok asked. I wanted to salute this guy.

'No I did not hear anyone screaming.' Mr Singh answered. Alok made a face and whispered in my ears:

'I know the murderer or he came here hiding his identity. Look at this' Alok said and showed me card of a salesman. The name was shocking. It was written: Mohan Pandey.

I took a deep breath and went to Ali.

'Alok I am very sorry to say but this murder is also done by the same serial killer we are looking for. Your wife was hit by some heavy metal rod or hammer on her head and after that he kept on attacking her until he was satisfied.' Ali said and added. 'I'm feeling very bad for you brother. I don't know why he killed her?'

'All you need to know is Mohan came here.' Ali was shocked after hearing Mohan's name.

'What??'

'Yes, look at this card. His name is written on it but peculiar thing is that this card doesn't have any company's name printed on it.' Ali looked at it as if he was holding Kohinoor diamond.

'Why Mohan will kill his wife?'

'We don't know.' Alok's face grew sadder. I understood if we stay here anymore, he would get into mess of crying again. I took Ali to a corner.

'I don't think he can handle it, any longer. We should leave.'

'What about his children?'

'I have told his neighbour to take proper care of them till he returns. Let me know if you get anything important. Ali, we can't afford to lose anything.' I said. Ali hugged

Alok. Alok did not participate. However, he did not have the energy to push him. Alok met his daughter and his son. They hugged him as they saw him.

'Where is mom?' His elder son asked him. Alok like a stony-hearted man brought a smile on his face. I look away.

'Mom is gone to her native place. She will return soon.'

'We will stay together from now onwards. Will we?' His son again questioned.

'Yes, my son after I come back. I have to complete an incomplete task.'

It was not like his kids were small. They were innocent. They were still not informed about their mother's death.

'You could have told them.' I said to Alok.

'I will.' He said and got into the police vehicle.

"DETECTIVE'S WIFE FOUND MURDERED"

The unfathomable mystery of four murders now has one new involvement of detective Alok Rajput's wife's murder. The police report says, Alok's wife Preeti has been murdered harshly with a heavy metalled substance.

This mystery of serial killings looks baffling.

Will Vikrant and Alok succeed in finding the fiend?

The last line read.

I ended reading this article, within no time. There were many allegations made against us, especially Alok regarding connections with the killer. Alok was busy on the table doing something. I sat there cursing various newspapers for starting my day, so badly. I needed one more cup of coffee but this was not my home. It was our office and we had limited stock left. I was too lazy to go out and bring something for me. Last night, I tried to chat to Alok about his wife's death but he ignored the topic by saying, "Discussion is not going to be helpful". Later at night, I also called Ali for updates. There were none. This case really looked unsolvable. I knew Alok was unhappy and was feeling worst but he was behaving normal. He can also be in a state of shock, I thought.

'Oh Shit!' Alok shouted. I went up to him and asked:

'Why did you shout?'

'How we missed this?'

'What are talking about?'

'Let me show you what I have got!' Alok exclaimed.

Alok and I had come for our secret meeting. No one knew about it. We were waiting at Lakshmi MisthanBhandar hotel, popularly just known as LMB. We came here to meet one person who was going to help us. Alok had almost solved the case. He came fifteen minutes after our arrival. We saw him in a muck sweat. He was wearing a formal shirt and pant. I ordered lassi for all of us. We talked about important matters related to the case. Alok explained him everything from the beginning.

'Are you sure?' He asked us.

'We are damn sure! He is the one...' I said with confidence.

'That's okay. If we go wrong regarding this, we can be in deep trouble. I know you both are right but still...' He stopped in middle. He was not yet confident.

'I know what you are thinking about. Don't worry. Everything will go according to Ali's plan. Ali's plan is superb. We will catch the killer.' I assured.

'Are you sure he will come after such tight arrangements by police department?' He asked.

'He will definitely come. He wants to kill us.' Alok replied this time.

He gave me a packet and I quietly kept it inside my bag. He left before us...

We sat there waiting for someone else...

Detective Vikrant Gupta's Narrative—IX

22/08/1972

I was feeling very different, on 22nd. When you know someone is going to kill you. You can't stay calm nor even act like that. Today was different. Firstly, I drank four cups of coffee in previous 3 hours. Secondly, Alok was talking a lot today. Ali was simply listening to us. He came exactly at 12am. As per murderer's record, he can murder anytime. There was one more thing I did not want: that is surprises from the murderer. If he shows up in an unexpected way then we all are gone. At 7, someone knocked on the main door. Ali went and opened it widely. One of his useless inspectors wanted to go home because his wife was ill. Totally, 10 police officers were around our office. Every passing minute gave me relief. However, I wasn't that worried but still death is something a human being is always afraid from. Ali had his revolver in his hand. Alok's second home was protected from all the corners. But there was silence. Silence because of fear...

'What I am feeling right now is just what a decent man would have felt after meeting a gay!' I tried to crack a joke. No one laughed instead of it they gave me are-you-mad look. Again silence took its place. Automatically I started thinking about this case:

What a confusing case is this? Murder, madness and serial killing, many more words can be attached to this case. Five murders, five notes, and only one bottle of blood gifted by someone to my best friend and still we are not sure about who is the murderer? Lastly, we are here at our office waiting for a person who will come to kill us.

Alok made another round of black tea, this time. I finished all the coffee powder.

'Don't you have coffee?' Ali asked Alok.

'He emptied the bottle.' I gave him a smile. *Drinking coffee is not a crime.*

Morning transformed into afternoon but no one came. Now the only time the murderer would come will, at night. One needs support of the darkness to kill two people. Anyways, Alok's second home was a bungalow and there was enough space to bury two people. Clouds of tiredness were moving over my mind. I hate afternoon with high temperature, I said to myself.

'There are things I'm worried about. What if he doesn't come?' Ali said while I was reading newspaper.

'Why are thinking so negative?' Alok responded.

'There is a clear possibility of it because you and Vikrant are protected. He is clever and we all know it. He can also change his plans.' Ali can also be right.

'He will come, Ali. I believe in him.'

'You believe in a criminal?'

'Yes' Alok sniffed. I was feeling bad for Alok. He still had to cremate his wife.

'How can you be sure about it?' I said not focusing on newspaper.

'Vikrant, he wants to put an end to our chapter. Mohan will come'

'Mohan' Ali almost shouted.

'Yes! We got his card from my home, dammit. He is a bloody asshole. Fucking swine', Alok abused Mohan and smashed his hand on a wooden table. Alok's action displayed his anger. 'I promise you, I will kill him'

'Alok, control yourself. Don't shout unnecessarily.' I said making him sit down.

'Mohan will come prepared. Just 4 hours from now. It will be dark.' Ali said.

I nodded. Lot of things were going to happen after four hours. I looked up. There was a shaft of sunlight. All of a sudden I don't what happened to me, but I started thinking about god. I believed in god. He is the one who made mankind and nature. It was not like, I loved him. I hated him too. I hated god for not giving everyone happiness in life. I always thought why god plans for us? He always does what he wants. What about us?

'Come in, Vikrant.' I heard Alok's voice from inside. Again, my question was left unanswered.

After 8pm, Alok's Second Home (Office)

'Something is wrong.' Alok said, suddenly. I was ready for my nap when Alok said. *Nice timing.*

'What?' I asked.

'Can you hear that noise?' I became extra attentive. The noise was coming from our washroom. Noise was of water flowing from the tap. I opened the door and closed the tap and I went inside the bedroom and turned on the tube lights. I wanted to take my tablets for headache. I found that tablet in five minutes. I was turning off the light of the bedroom and at the same time I saw a shadow. It was of a man. My heart was almost going to fail. I drew a quick breath and stepped towards the drawing room. I couldn't move because someone was holding me from back. I looked back. I saw he was pointing a gun towards me. He looked familiar. I knew him. He was someone I had defeated long back, during my times. This time it is his chance to punish me. Mohan was glaring at me with his green eyes. I looked down as he pushed me towards the drawing room. Alok and Ali both look equally shocked. They looked at me and Mohan as if we were aliens. Trust me: my heartbeat was faster than ever...

'Leave him, I said' Ali hollered at Mohan.

'Do you think I will leave him? Now please, I kindly request you to keep your fucking revolver on that table.' Mohan said, clasping my both the hands. Ali kept his pistol on the table and lifted both arms above his head.

'Leave me, you peace of shit' I slowly whispered in his ears.

'Huh? You will happy leaving this world, right?' Mohan said and laughed.

'No!' I shouted.

Mohan was taller and me. Mohan told, Ali to stick to one corner and direct me and Alok to another one. Ali and

I were parallel to each other. Mohan took Ali's pistol and tucked in his pant.

'Why you killed my wife?' Alok screamed. Someone knocked the door.

'Open it and tell your officers to quietly stay outside otherwise I will shoot one of them.' Mohan said pointing his pistol on us. Ali's team came inside in a style with five revolvers pointed towards Mohan. Mohan shook his head looking at Ali.

'Go outside', Ali said and blinked his eyes twice. Mohan did not notice it. They closed the door. Mohan took a chair and sat on it. I was looking straight into his eyes. 'Why you killed my Preeti?' Alok shouted again. Mohan looked at him and said:

'I murdered your wife because of you!' Mohan retorted, pointing his fingers towards me.

'What was her fault?' I said.

'I wanted to kill someone from your family! But you became an unmarried ashole detective with nothing to lose. I wanted to kill someone close to you so that you would get hurt. I got an idea of murdering Alok but he was out of my range because he was with you and it was not that easy to plan his murder. So, I killed his wife. By the way, how do you know that I killed his wife?' He said and laughed. Alok looked at me as if I were his enemy. He did not say anything. I felt guilty.

'What about other murders?' I asked him, angrily.

'Look down you cunt otherwise...' Mohan said and fired a bullet up on the ceiling. Immediately, I looked down. I was afraid. We were in deep trouble. We needed help. The one who had come to help us was in a corner, with his hands up. There was no time to think about how he came here. The major problem was—he has come here.

'This is what I call happiness. Vikrant, look how time has changed, you are like a slave and I am like your master. Years back, you made me run like a dog and see now I am so powerful that even a police officer is helpless. Times changes Vikrant but people never forget their past.' I wanted to kill him, right now.

'Mohan if you wanted to murder us then why you killed others? What was their fault?' I yelled.

'Their fault was—they supported you. I never wanted to kill them. Whenever, I hear people admiring you and your work, my heart burns. My friends say I am jealous of you.' Mohan stammered. 'In that feeling I killed people. I never wanted to kill anyone but it just happened. After so many years, I got a chance to kill take my revenge. That is why I started everything. From the first murder to the last, I have killed only random people I met on that particular date. Public supports you and they also trust you, what about me, huh? I stay in Jaipur and listen them talking about you. I feel worst.' Mohan roared. He was not alright. Jealousy had created a negative patch on his mind. He only wanted me dead. The anger which he had stored inside him for years made him do these murders. The simple reason behind this case was—dislike. He never liked me.*Why a criminal would like me?*

'Mohan you are mentally ill. You need to visit a psychiatrist?' Dumb Ali asked him. Mohan laughed.

'What? Are you taking me for granted? I'm here to kill both of them. I am not a psychopath. I am a normal person who is behaving like a lunatic because of this fucking Vikrant.' Mohan said showing his anger.

'Do you think you defeated me?' I said standing up.

'Yes'

'Today, also I am more powerful than you! I have thousands of people who love me. They won't stop loving me owing to the fact that I was murdered by a maniac.' I laughed. 'I won'

Mohan got up from his seat and smashed my head on the wall. Blood started flowing from my head. I tried to grab the revolver but he was too muscular for me. He kicked me and gave a punch on my face. I pushed him into a corner that is when Ali and Alok joined the fight. Ali pushed him and finally Alok took Mohan's revolver in his hand. Mohan had another revolver tucked in his pant. He took it out and pointed towards us. We were three and he was alone.

'You still have time, you can surrender.' Ali asked him to give up.

'Fuck you' He said and fired a bullet towards Ali. Ali somehow dodged it. Three of us, then jumped on him and started kicking every part of his body. Mohan's both the revolvers were now in our possession. I kicked on his butt. Mohan was shouting some nonsense… "You will have to pay for it…" We ignored his words. Ali opened the main door and told his team to arrest him.

'So, congratulations to you for your victory.' Alok said to him. He looked up and said:

'One day, I will definitely kill you both.'

'One day, after months, you will be hanged. Mohan you could have been a good person. Life gave you a second chance but did not utilize it properly. Now you will have to pay for your sins.' I said to him.

'It depends on me what I want to do. Crime is in my blood, Vikrant.' Mohan barked.

'Whatever. Take him.' Ali said to his team. He had a smile on his face.

'At last, we solved the case. What a big relief!' Ali said to us.

I went to the bedroom and brought a towel to clean blood from my head. It was unbearably paining. Alok was still not talking to me. *He must be thinking I am responsible for his wife's death. Am I?*

I drank water and glanced at the wall clock. It showed—10pm. I was feeling hungry. I went to the kitchen and grabbed an apple to satisfy my hunger. Alok was reading something when I went to him. I kept my hand on his right shoulder. 'I am sorry' I said.

'It is not your fault.' I looked down to see what he was reading.

Promise me, Alok. You will never leave
any chapter of your life incomplete.

These words were written on that paper. I looked at him. His eyes had tears. I was observing him. I was feeling bad for him when someone knocked on the main door.

DETECTIVE VIKRANT GUPTA'S NARRATIVE—X

We looked up and saw something unthinkable. Ali was standing at the door with his revolver directed towards us. It was unimaginable. But it was true.

'Stop being funny and keep that revolver down.' I said and laughed. He did not.

'I am not a joker, Vikrant.' He said.

'I know, Ali. I know everything except one bloody thing.' Alok said, fiercely.

Yes! Ali was behind every murder. Mohan was just the first part of his whole plan. Second part was remaining, yet. We saw a different, Ali. Ali killed everyone.

'Your game is over, Ali.' I said.

'You mean yours'

'No.' I said and opened the window on my left side. There he was. Sanjay Jaiswal came in by jumping over. Ali was shocked to see him. Sanjay Jaiswal also brought his team of two people with him, they were head inspectors and shoot out specialist too. Within, no time Ali was arrested by them.

'So will you say it yourself or should we?' Sanjay Jaiswal asked Ali.

'No, I have not committed any crime. I am innocent.'

'We have caught you red-handed, Ali.'

'Do you have any proof?' Ali said and laughed. He laughed louder. Sanjay looked at us.

'I will explain everything and I also have evidence.' Ali's laughter therapy stopped. Ali's face became a serious one. He glared at me. *Impossible*: he must be thinking. Alok went in the bedroom and brought a file. He opened it.

'This case was of murders, mysteries and one manipulator. When the first letter arrived, Ali told us that one unknown man came and handed that letter to his constable who is a lazy ass. He never told us to interrogate him or even ask him who that unknown man was because no man gave any letter to any constable. It was a lie told by him to us. The letter was written by Ali himself. The letter was written in a different style and with different hand writing. Ali wanted us to take that letter seriously. The letter was news of someone's death which was written by Rakesh. I and Vikrant started calculating possibilities related to the letter. We ended up with nothing. At night, police got a dead body of an old man. He was Harish Chandra. Ali killed him just as a start. He was old and had no power so Ali killed him easily. So, smartly he left another letter (second letter) in the pocket of that victim (Harish Chandra). When we reached the crime scene, Ali told us to come with him. He did not let us stay there for a while. Ali took us to the police station and told us about the second letter. That is when our thinking came up to a madman. We all thought there is a man who has gone mad and is killing everyone. Still we were not satisfied. Well, Ali had his plans ready. Then I and Vikrant went to Harish's house and at his workplace. Everyone said he was a very good man. Our question was: why anyone would kill a decent old man? I don't know from where but unexpectedly Ali got the information about Harish's evil acts. He told us, Harish supplied girls. We believed him. Second murder happened on the written date, 12th August. This time a girl from Maharani Girls College was found murdered on the streets. Like previous murder, this girl was also killed brutally with a hammer. I was pretty sure this was also done by the same killer. Ali did it easily. He first kidnapped Akanksha in the morning and kept her in some silent area for a while. After sometime, he killed her. Ali did not let us investigate on this murder. Ali also told us about Akanksha being a call girl. Ali also showed us the letter for the third murder. This time he had mentioned, mine and Vikrant's name in it. I don't know why it sounded challenging? After both crimes—we still did not have any evidence. We came to a conclusion that the murderer is gone mad and is killing people who are destroying our society and culture. We had something that day. Next murder happened, on 15th August. This time also victim was a woman, her name was Ambika Parmar. Style of murdering was the same. Ali was in tension that day. We thought it was because of press meeting but it was not that simple.' Alok coughed twice. I gave me a glass of water.

'When Ali was killing Ambika accidently her brother (Ajit) saw Ali. He was afraid if he complains it to police.

So he kept him somewhere in private. Ali had many such contacts. After the meeting, Ali told us; Ambika took donations for admissions and after taking money she did not gave poor people seat. Ambika also had political connections. Then a startling thing happened. One of police constables found Ajit's body on the rear side of the police station. We were all shocked. Later we understood the reason behind it. When Ali was coming to police station he must have killed him. It was easy for him to carry a dead body. That is when we got our death note.' Alok stopped.

'Now you say, Ali' Alok said pointing his finger towards him.

'I never committed any crime. These guys are just blaming me without evidence.' Ali yelled.

'I can try to explain but I am not sure about it', I said. 'Can you?'

'Yes.' Alok and Sanjay both nodded. Go on, Vikrant, I said to myself.

'He somehow must have contacted Mohan because Ali knew Mohan disliked me. So, he made a plan with him. Mohan and Ambika had an affair some 10 years back. Mohan was a born criminal and Ambika got to know about him. Ambika left Mohan because his business was illegal (kidnapping). This thing left Mohan's heart broken. He wanted to take his revenge. So, Mohan told Ali to murder Ambika because according to Ali's plan he wanted to put all our attention to Mohan instead of the murderer. So, when we went to Ambika's apartment. Ali intentionally showed us the photograph of Ambika and Mohan together. After further investigation, doubt against Mohan increased. That is when we got a parcel at

Alok's this home. Parcel contained a bottle of blood with a sticky note. When we went to check at his apartment, we found his wife murdered harshly. Still Alok kept his heart strong and he somehow discovered a salesman's card. The name of the salesman was—Mohan Pandey. Ali murdered Alok's wife and kept Mohan's card so that everyone will doubt Mohan. Master stroke, it was.' I explained.

'What rubbish you are talking about?' Ali said.

'It is the truth.' I declared.

'Do you have any evidence?'

'Yes, I have.' This time it was Alok.

Alok pulled out the drawer and showed us a squared paper.

'What is this?' Sanjay Jaiswal asked. Alok came forward and showed it everyone.

1st Letter:

"I know you.Very well"

2nd Letter:

"I will be gifting you a dead body"

3rd Letter:

"I am very close to you"

'I was lucky to get this small piece of paper. Look at the words, of 1st and the 3rd letter. They easily prove that Ali has done these murders. He knows us, very well and he is very close to us. Apart from the words, the most identical thing is…' Alok went towards the table and quickly grabbed the documents over there. 'I compared the handwriting of these letters with this paper. I found it exactly the same.'

Sanjay took the papers in his hand and made a serious face and started observing both the papers as if his eyes had magnifying lens. He then looked up and returned it to Alok. Ali sat there shocked and surprised.

'You're right! By the way, where you got this piece of paper from?' Alok smiled.

'Ali gave me his book, "Great Expectations". I got this from middle pages of that book.' I laughed.

'That means he solved his own case.' Sanjay replied with a smile.

'Case is not yet solved!' Alok said. *What's remaining?*

'Why you killed Preeti? Why you wanted to kill us?' Alok asked him in a firm voice.

'You have defeated me again and again, Alok. Today, as well goes to you.'

'Me?' Alok said, confused. *Again and again, I thought.*

'Yes!' Ali sniffed. Alok and I took our seats to listen him.

'I loved Preeti. When I was in college, Preeti and I were in a relationship. We were happy and satisfied. But one day, out of the blue, Preeti and his family shifted to Mumbai from Jaipur. I tried to contact Preeti but I was not successful in it. I was left, dejected. I stopped doing everything. I stopped my studies. I became an alcoholic. When I was hopeless, I joined police. I worked there like a dog. I intentionally took on training. I went too hard on myself. Years later, I saw Preeti again. I thought she was back. I tried to meet her. But I rarely spotted her. But one day I thought a chance to meet her privately. I told her everything about myself. What I did without her? Why I became a police officer? What is my salary? Everything. When I started talking about our future, she stepped back. She told me a bitter truth: She was married. I decided. I will never talk to her, again. Still Preeti had a tight grip on me. Days were killing me, from inside. Negative thoughts started to develop in my brain. Those days, Vikrant introduced me to you. We became friendly and enjoyed working together. Vikrant started spending more time with you, like a brother. Earlier he used to spend most of his evenings with me. We were like brothers. Suddenly, it seemed like the whole world was against me. After some days, I got to know you were Preeti's husband. I got extremely angry. Preeti married to a loser like you. I decided to propose Preeti for marriage. I went to your home and proposed her. Preeti slapped me and tossed the gift which I had brought for her out of the window. She insulted me just because she was married. I thought about it a lot. I told myself, it was not her mistake. It was your fault. That day, I knew you were here; I went to your home. I told Preeti that you were dead and now she can freely marry me. She slapped me right across my face. I don't know what happened to me? But I killed her. Love died that day. Alok you've fucked me all my life. You took my brother away from me and took my girl too. That is the reason behind this whole case.' Ali completed his story.

Alok was in tears. Suddenly, Alok got up and went inside. I ran behind him. Alok took out a gun from the packet.   'Alok' I shouted from behind as he was returning to drawing room. He went and pointed that gun towards Ali.

'No, Alok. I gave you this gun for self-defence.' Sanjay said.

'Some people deserve to die.' Alok said and fired a bullet on his stomach.

Ali did not cry. Ali was laughing as he fell on the floor. Sanjay took the gun from Alok. Ali laughed.

'Why are you laughing?' Alok asked him.

'This is going to make me even more powerful. I surrender myself to evil...' Ali said something in other laugh and continued. 'I put a curse on this land. Whoever will come here, will never go alive.' Ali muttered maledictions loudly. After few minutes, Ali died. Sanjay, I and Alok had only one thing to do. Cremate his body...

Sanjay told everyone Alok fired a bullet in self-defense. Sanjay assured us, nothing will happen to Alok. Though I never liked Sanjay but that day I felt real likeness for him. That day, I realized there is nothing called as prefect crime. But crimes can be near to perfection. Ali wanted us to chase a madman and then Mohan. He had almost outsmarted us. Luckily, we found a way.

"DETECTIVE ALOK RAJPUT IS MASTER IN SOLVING IMPOSSIBLE CASES"

The headlines read.

PART THREE

CHAPTER TEN

It was a refreshing weather at Shimla. There were people who got out of their houses early for the day's work. It was still dark outside. There was darkness in Neha's life too. Vikrant completed narrating his story. Neha couldn't believe her ears. It was a new lesson for Neha. She was surprised by two facts. First, her grandfather was a detective. Second, her grandfather betrayed her. Neha was confused about how to feel. She had mixed up her mind. On one hand, she wanted love her grandfather for doing such great work and on the other hand she wanted to hate him for gifting her that land. Ali was the evil spirit who resided on that land. Neha was bewildered and tired.

'Why did he give that land to me?' Neha asked Vikrant. Vikrant tried to speak and started coughing and spluttering. Neha made a face looking at him.

'I don't know. Last time, when we met he told me, that land is the only property he is left with. He did not mention about specially gifting it to you. He had to give to someone before dying so he gave it to you.'

'Grandpa should have told me the truth. At least...' Neha broke down in tears. Neha would have been with Ashish if Alok told her the truth before.

'Neha, I know what you must be feeling right now. I am not married but I understand. There must be a reason behind it. Alok never did things, idly. Well, I have something to show you.' Vikrant said and opened his case file and removed a paper from it. Neha wiped her face with a handkerchief.

'What is this?'

'He gave this paper to me in 2011. Take a look.' Vikrant handed that paper to Kusum.

> I know I have done a mistake, a big mistake. I killed Ali because he killed Preeti. It was my aggressive part. That time, when Ali was sayingevil things to evil. I ignored him and thought it was all nonsense.

> In the year, 1973 I started observing many paranormal activities. I met people who... knew about it and told them about it. They advised me to leave that house soon. I did as I they said.

> From the year, 1974 to 1978—I faced many problems related to my life and family. I was alone and helpless. My son's accident and my daughter failing in exams, and

I lost my job too. I was surrounded by problems and I lacked solutions to those problems.

In the year 1999, my son and his wife died in an accident. It was the second big loss of my life. When I came home from his funeral, it seemed like I was possessed by someone. Inside me, some other person was talking. The person who had possessed me told; he will never let my family members live in peace. He will ruin my future generation.When I came back to my senses, I remembered every word what he said. I was worried about my future. Was he behind my son's accident? I wondered.

In the year, 2002 in February I got a call from an unknown number. It was a late night call after 12pm. I ignored at first. But the caller started irritating me by calling again and again. When I picked up the call I got to know it was not a normal call. Ali's spirit contacted me. He only said; "I will extirpate your family". I was not sure about me or my family's future.

Ali's spirit was free and was destroying my family. One day, no one in my family would be alive. Legacy of Rajput's will end soon. Negative thoughts started making a space in my mind. Will Rajputs die soon? I am writing this because I want someone from my family to fight against Ali's spirit. I know it will be hard. I know it can be impossible. But trust me; Rajput's are the one who make the impossible, possible. I believe in our blood. I believe in my future generation. Mostly, for now I don't believe in myself.

Alok Rajput

It was one of the last letters by Alok. He mentioned his problems and he also mentioned what problems his future generation can face. He myself would have fought with him but problems didn't allow him. It was painful for him to know the future of his family. One day, everyone in Rajput family would die. In reality, only Kusum and Neha were left. No one else was remaining.

'He wants us to fight against, Ali.' Kusum said after reading the letter. Vikrant was observing both of them.

'He is a powerful evil spirit and who we are?' Neha questioned.

'What do you mean, Neha?'

'I mean to say is, how are we going to fight against someone who is not visible to us? He can come in us and go. He can do anything.'

'Stop, arguing. Can I say something?' Vikrant realized fight was going to start soon so he interrupted them.

'You will have to fight against, Ali otherwise one day you will also die. You have no option. I know it is hard when it comes to evil spirits and all. I have never met any evil spirit in my life. There are methods to get rid of evil spirits attached to you. I think you should search for a spiritualist. They know how to deal with spirits.' Vikrant wanted Neha and Kusum to be safe.

'I'm sorry. I am only talking about the negatives leaving possibilities of positives.' Neha said, yawning.

'You must be tired. Go and get some sleep.' Vikrant advised both of them. Neha and Kusum also needed some rest. Sometimes what one needs is a good piece of advice.

Neha's life had always been flooded with problems. After her parent's death, she almost had no one in her life. Of course Kusum was there for her but Neha missed her parents anyways. Now, Neha understood why she faced problems in her earlier life? Why she lost her parents? She had got the answer she was searching for. Neha knew that Ali was the evil spirit in that house. Now all she needed was enough courage to fight against Ali's spirit. Worried Neha slept with no idea about her future.

Vikrant wanted to help Neha but he himself needed help at his age. He thought to support Neha by searching a real spiritualist for her. There were people who were false and had no power to communicate with evil. They fooled people for money. Vikrant didn't want Neha to be cheated by these people. Neha was already depressed. Vikrant was residing in Shimla from almost 8 years. He had enough contacts to deal with any problem. One of his close friends gave him the number of a spiritualist.

'I want to tell you. I have searched for a spiritualist. His name is Peter.'

'Is he real?' Kusum also knew about malpractices carried on by fake people.

'He is real. My friends have heard about him.' Vikrant said. He looked at Neha. Neha was lost in her world. She did not want to communicate with others.

'Neha' Vikrant called out.

'I heard.' Neha said.

Neha was feeling guilty about killing her own husband. She was killing herself from inside. When she needed to be strong, she was falling apart. That is what people call— evil effect. Ali wanted to kill her slowly.

CHAPTER ELEVEN

It was a bad morning for Suresh. He had an important work in bank and he was already late for work. He was shouting at his wife for not preparing breakfast on time. He was irritated and angry. Suresh stepped out of his house. When he was starting his car, he saw Riya coming from ahead. She was sweating.

'Ashish and Neha are not there in their house.' Riya said as she came near him.

'What? Where did they go in a night?' Suresh got out from his car.

'I am extremely anxious about them. Do you think something bad has happened to them?'

'Nothing will happen to them. I won't let anything happen to her.' Suddenly, Suresh became protective for Neha. Suresh forgot all his work and started thinking about Neha. Riya noticed quick change in Suresh's expression.

'You won't let anything happen to her. Am I hearing it from Suresh, himself?' Riya said doubting him.

'I am just saying. Do you want anything bad to happen?' Riya shook her head.

'Before we start panicking about them, try to call them. Do you have their number?'

'No' Riya responded negatively. Both of them didn't have their number.

'Let's go' Suresh said and strolled towards Neha and Ashish's house. Riya had no choice but to follow him.

When Suresh reached near their house, he swiftly told Riya to stop and alone went inside. He checked if the door was locked or not. It was locked. He signalled Riya to come inside the gate and both of them went to the backside of the bungalow. Suresh looked around. He got nothing. Suresh and Riya returned to the front side.

'We can't do anything. The door is locked and no windows are open.' Suresh said to Riya.

'Were you figuring out the way to sneak inside their house?'

'Yes!'

'What an idea!' Riya frowned. Suresh understood why she did that.

'Or else we can just wait for them to come back.'

'What if they don't come back ever?' Suresh was searching for an appropriate answer when he saw Ashish coming from the rear side. He was happy to see him, okay. Riya too saw him and called out for him.

'Where were you and Neha? We are searching for you both.' Riya noticed his clothes were covered with mud as if he was swimming in a muddy pool. 'Why are your clothes splattered by mud?'

'I was watering plants that side. Suddenly from where I don't know a cat jumped on me. I lost my balance and fell down.' Ashish said in a dull voice. Riya noticed something in him.

'Where is Neha?'

'She has gone to the market.' Ashish said, scraping his elbow.

'Why you wanted to meet us?'

'Just came to see if everything is fine.' Suresh said hiding the actual reason.

'What the hell is going to happen to us?' Ashish yelled at him. Suresh did not answer to him.

'When Neha will come back? I want to meet her.'

'She may come in 2 or 3 hours.' Ashish answered and said, 'Okay'

'I will come to meet her in the afternoon.' Riya said and they both left.

'I saw something strange in him' Riya informed Suresh.

'What are you talking about?'

'I can't describe it. Something strange I saw' she answered.

Suresh looked back. He was unable to spot Ashish.

Ashish unlocked the door and went inside.Ashish wasn't alive. Ashish's dead body was walking.Someone was using his body. Someone.

At 2pm, Riya reached their house to meet Neha. Riya really felt it was now very important to meet her. Riya was a strong woman but she also had feelings. She just wanted to ensure that Neha is okay. Riya herself had a headache. She needed some good rest but after meeting Neha. When she reached their house, she saw the house was locked from outside. "What the fuck!" she abused the situation which was in front of her. She immediately started worrying about Neha. Riya was thinking of going home when she heard a noise from inside the house. Riya followed the voice and stopped near a window. She looked inside the house through transparent glass.

She saw Ashish was at home. But the door was locked from outside. Ashish was ranting something loudly. She went more near to the window trying to hear him.

'I will kill her. Let her come here, again. I am the most powerful spirit here. No one can do anything to me. I worship evil and his powers. God cannot do anything to me. There is always a fight between god and evil and every time god wins. This time, I will make myself proud. Every time I worship you, I become more and more strong and undefeatable. This time no one will defeat me. I will win. I will win.' Riya heard Ashish saying this. Riya's heartbeat quickened as she saw Ashish looking towards her. She screamed and ran outside the house. She looked at the house. Suddenly, entrance door opened. Riya became attentive. Ashish came out and smiled at her. She stepped back. Riya realized Ashish was coming towards her. She took another step back. Ashish stopped and said:

'Next time don't come inside this gate. Otherwise you will be like him, dead.' Ashish said pointing his forefinger towards himself.

'Huh?' Horror-struck, she stared at him with frightening eyes. She did not speak a single word. Riya had no courage to talk to a dead person.

'Okay?' he said. Riya slowly nodded. He went back while Riya was still mulling over what she saw few minutes back. It did not happen with her earlier. She had never heard something of that kind from anyone. Even in

T.V serials they did not show such gruesome things. Riya called Suresh.

'We need to talk.' Riya said.

'Why?' Suresh responded. Riya was already shocked by what she had seen in addition to it Suresh was questioning to her.

'Don't ask questions. Just come over my place.' Riya said and ended the call.

Ashish is dead, Riya thought. *Who killed him?*

'What the fuck are you babbling?' Suresh yelled like a mad person. Riya told him, everything she heard and saw. 'You mean he is dead, really?'

'Yes, he himself told me. It was not him.'

'What?' Suresh asked, puzzled.

'Someone was inside him. Someone was controlling him. How can a dead man walk otherwise?' Riya said.

'This problem has become more complicated.'

'What do you think? Should we call a priest?' Riya asked him.

'Okay. But where is Neha?' Suresh's question echoed in Riya's mind. They both looked at each other. On the other hand, someone was waiting for Neha, desperately.

CHAPTER TWELVE

Peter Fernandez was born at a bus stop; his family had no money to take his mother in the hospital. Peter's earlier life only consisted of struggles and hard work. When Peter was eleven years old, he met a churchman of a famous church. He told him, "You're god gifted". Peter was young and in his routine, he forgot what the churchman said. At the age of 20, Peter realized about his powers. When he read bible or any other holy book, he felt that he was able to communicate with god. Whenever he wanted to take decisions, he communicated with god for answers. His questions were answered by god. Initially, no one believed him. He believed in helping people but people he wanted to help demoralized him. Later on people started appreciating him and respected him. He never showed conceit while helping people during their bad times. Luckily, one day he again met that churchman. This time he said something else to him. He told him, "Listen my son, there is always a positive part and a negative part.

God cannot be everywhere. So he created many helping hands. Son, you are one of them. You can communicate with god and you can also communicate with dead. You can help people who are suffering because of evil powers in this world. You're a savior, my son." Peter Fernandez never saw himself as a savior. Peter's power increased with time. He could hear strange voices and screams of people. He could feel one's pain.

'Are you Peter Fernandez?' Neha approached him. Kusum accompanied Neha. Vikrant did not come.

'Yes I'm Peter Fernandez. You must be Neha, right?' Peter said. Peter could help himself noticing Neha's beauty. She was the most beautiful woman he had ever seen. Neha nodded.

'Vikrant sir said it is about some evil spirit who is trying to kill you.'

'Yes. Wait I will tell you everything.' Neha explained everything to him in short. Meanwhile, Peter was constantly looking at Neha. He liked her expressions, her lips, her nose, and her hair, everything about her.

'We can't talk about it, here. We need to go home.' Neha and Kusum agreed and followed him.

Peter's house was an old one, occupied with less furniture. Peter gave them tea and biscuits.

'Neha I am very sorry to hear about your husband's death. So, Neha how will you kill an evil spirit?'

'That is something which you should know.' Neha was confused about what Peter was talking.

'I don't kill anyone, Neha. I can only communicate with them.' Peter clarified.

'I don't know anything about these negative powers.' Neha said.

'We need to get rid of him as soon as possible. He is a trouble for us.' Kusum said. Peter was trying to read Neha's mind. The only thing which Peter understood by Neha's mind was pain. She was in extreme pain.

'It is not that easy. Let me explain you everything whatever I know. There are many psychologies related to ghost, devil and all. But I don't think anyone of those is a true one.' Neha frowned. Peter ignored her and continued. 'Now I will explain what I believe in. When a person dies, there is some kind of highly charged energy which comes out a person's body. After the death, body of a person has nothing to do with it. That energy which comes out of a person's body is responsive and conscious. That conscious energy is powerful to enter another cycle of life. There is a life after death. It is not like no one knows about it. But people don't believe in it. It is a mysterious thing. In that life, everyone is a free spirit. People's spirit can move around everywhere and can do anything. Like in your case, because of your grandfather's mistake you are suffering. People can take revenge after death because they live another life after death. They are invisible. Ali is powerful and invisible. That is why I asked you, how are you going to defeat him?' Peter explained them everything. Neha had no answer. Peter looked at Neha's blank face.

'We don't know. You can only guide us.' Kusum said.

'Before you do anything I would like to ask you, are you mentally strong?' Peter asked Neha.

'I think so. I am still trying to recover.' Neha coaxed.

'Good. You will need to be strong mentally. These evil spirits easily get over people who are mentally weak.

Your husband was brave, so he attacked you. They always attack the weaker one. Come inside my room.' He said and directed Neha towards his special room.

That room was unique from every room. There were 10 tube lights in that room. Peter switched on all the lights. Neha found it harder to keep her eyes open.

'Why there are so many tube lights?' Neha questioned him.

'I am going to communicate with, Ali's spirit. I keep this room bright. Evil powers feel weak when they come in brightness.' Peter said. Peter brought bible and kept it on a table. Neha was standing and observing his preparations before calling a spirit. Peter was finally ready with a bible, a large silver crucifix and one blank paper.

'Come on let's start.' Kusum and Neha both looked at each other having no idea about what will happen next? Peter told Neha to sit between him and Kusum. They all took their seats.

'Now listen to me carefully, Ali's spirit will come in your body, Neha. He will talk to us by using your physical body. In simple words, he will possess you to communicate with us.' Peter said.

'No, let Ali's spirit come to my body. I am also a Rajput.' Kusum said concerned about Neha.

'No aunty, let me do this. I want to know how powerful he is.' Neha said and looked at Kusum. After a long fifteen argument, Kusum gave up on stubborn Neha.

'Look Neha, you need to be mentally strong. He will capture your mind within no time.' Peter warned Neha.

"I need to be strong!" Neha kept saying to herself.

Peter kept the Bible aside. Peter then closed his eyes and started saying something in an inaudible voice. Neha and Kusum both looked at him as if he himself was an evil spirit. They quietly sat there in silence before Neha got a sudden jerk. Peter and Kusum both noticed it.

'Neha are you okay?' Kusum asked.

'Don't call me, Neha.' Neha responded. It was someone from Neha's body who was responding.

'What is your name?' Peter asked.

'My name is Ali' Kusum and Peter were now sure Neha was possessed by Ali.

'What do you want?'

'You called me here; you say what do you want?'

'Why are you troubling her?' Peter was saying slowly. Before Ali could respond, Kusum said:

'Why are you doing this to us? Please I beg, leave us. Let us live.' Ali laughed.

'You did not answer me.' Suddenly, Ali got up from his seat and sat on the table. He looked at Peter's eyes. He kept staring into Peter's eyes.

'I want to kill her.' This Peter began to laugh. *Everyone was laughing.*

'Who gave the permission to kill, anyone? Otherwise, I will...' Peter said and picked up the crucifix. He held it in front of Neha's body. Suddenly, her body began to shiver.

'Don't try it with me. I am very powerful to fight against.' Ali said.

'There is only one great power on this earth. That is power of god.' Peter shouted.

'Do you think you called me here? I came here myself.' Suddenly, all the tube lights switched off! Kusum started screaming. Peter told her not to.Possessed Neha got up from that table and took a pen. Neha was writing something. Ali's spirit left her body after writing a note.

When lights turned on Neha was seating on the chair, she was previously seating on. Peter and Kusum both gave her time to settle down. 'Are you okay?' Kusum asked her.

'Yes I think so.' Neha replied. Peter took that paper and read the written matter in his mind.

'You want to read.' Peter asked her. She nodded.

Something went wrong when Neha was possessed by Ali. Neha felt it. Neha knew it.

CHAPTER THIRTEEN

I am going to kill her. No one can stop me. Not even your god. Just remember one thing, the day she enters her house. She would become an intangible spirit like me. This time it is my chance to show my cleverness. Neha is paying for Alok's mistake.

Neha noticed it was written in a clumsy handwriting. Neha was tired. Neha was feeling drained.

'I think we should leave. I am already worn out.' Neha said in a low volume.

'It happens.' Peter admitted.

Neha thanked him and stepped out of his house. Fresh air made her feel good. Neha was feeling a different kind of energy in her. She was feeling light after meeting Peter. His appearance had somewhat given her confidence to fight against Ali. Neha was thinking about what she heard when she was possessed by Ali. There was something different. Many thoughts were rotating in her mind: what the hell was happening there? He told me something. I remember it, nicely. But I don't want to believe it. I cannot even know if it is true or not.

'What are you thinking?' Kusum asked her on the way.

'I can't say anything right now.' Neha did not want anyone to know about it.

'What are we going to do next?'

'I forgot to tell you. I am going to Jaipur, tomorrow.' Neha answered.

'Are you serious?'

'Yes'

'Are you gone mad? You know Ali there...' Neha cut her voice off and said:

'So what if Ali's spirit is there in that house? I don't' fear him, anymore.' Kusum was surprised by seeing Neha's courage. A girl who was afraid of talking about an evil spirit a day before was now not scared of anyone. Neha needed only one thing to do now. Meet Vikrant and leave.

There are secrets which should not be told to anyone. Not even family. Neha had one such secret, now.

Evil spirits, even if they are not near they have the power to spoil things. The same thing was happening with Neha. Though Neha was feeling better but she was still racked with pain. She decided to go to Jaipur a day after. Neha needed time for herself. Neha avoided thinking about Ashish. She understood she couldn't live in pain. Kusum too was distressed. Instead of motivating Neha, she locked herself in a room with loneliness and grief. But Neha wanted to keep herself motivated and strong enough to fight against Ali's spirit.

It was night time and it is believed that during moon light, people see ghost. Vikrant was sitting in a deckchair on the lawn when he saw Neha coming towards him. Neha looked depressed.

'Are you not sleeping?' Vikrant asked her.

'I don't want to sleep. Whenever I sleep I remember that sin which I committed. I feel horrible.'

'It is a sin but you did not do it. You were not in your senses when you stabbed the knife in Ashish's stomach. You're not guilty in the eyes of God. Trust me, you're not.' Vikrant said. Neha looked up and said:

'I don't understand on thing. Why this Ali's spirit is only after me? Why is he not troubling you? You too helped grandpa to catch him.' Neha had a point.

'I don't know. I helped him in some ways. He is after your family because he hated Alok. Ali also loved Preeti, your grandmother. Ali was like my brother. But the way he murdered people, he deserved to die.' Vikrant said and rub his hands. It was an icy-cold night.

'Do you think what grandpa did was right?' Neha needed answers to her questions. Vikrant found it harder to answer her. He was a good man. He did not want to take anyone's side.

'Why are you asking?'

'I need to your opinion.' Neha snapped.

'Alok was a priggish person. He did things which he felt were right. Alok did right.' Vikrant opined.

'These superior talks don't help in real life. I lost my life partner.'

'He too lost his life, partner.' Vikrant said. 'It was his past, Neha'

'Yes! Grandpa's past and my present are inextricable.' Neha said.

Neha went inside the house leaving Vikrant outside. Vikrant found it weird.

'Are you okay?' Vikrant asked as he stood at the door of Neha's room. Neha was rearranging her clothes in the bag. 'Come in, sir.' Vikrant sat. Vikrant wanted to talk to Neha about her plan. In the afternoon, Neha told Kusum and Vikrant about her decision that she was going back to Jaipur, to stay in her house. Vikrant did not say anything at that point of time. Neha packed her bags, properly.

'Are you going to Jaipur tomorrow?'

'Yes, tomorrow I am leaving Shimla.' Neha said and smiled. There was awkwardness flying in the air. Vikrant's face defined his concern for her. Vikrant never married anyone but he was an emotional person. He also had a dream of having a family but his secret work deprived him from having a family. He looked at Neha from his blue eyes.

'You can stay here as long as you want. If you don't want to go, stay here forever. I don't want anything to happen to you. Alok was a family. He never treated me as an outsider or a stranger. I don't want you to die, like him. So, what I am saying is, think about the decision you've made.' Neha could see tears in Vikrant's eyes. The bond which Alok and Vikrant shared was immortal and unbreakable. Neha understood Vikrant treated her like his daughter.

'I can't spend here my whole life. I am an independent girl. I have made the right decision, I think. Living a courageous life is way better than a fearful one. I know sir you care for me and feel that I am your daughter.

But you and grandpa both are brave and bold. I'm his granddaughter. How do you expect me to run away from this situation? Where my family's future is at stake? I won't let it happen, sir.' Neha said, bravely.

'Don't call me sir. Call me grandpa.' Vikrant said and hugged Neha tightly. It was an emotional moment. Vikrant broke down and wept. Neha held him, tightly and whispered in his ears:

'Don't cry grandpa. I will be okay.' Vikrant felt blessed.

'What are you going to do about Ali?' Vikrant asked Neha after their emotional session.

'I cannot say anything right now. I have not decided any plan or procedure related to it.' Neha lied.

'What do mean by that? You're going to deal an evil spirit. Not any human. Take any priest with you for your safety. You cannot fight with him alone.' He advised.

'I don't need anyone. Kusum aunty is also not going to come with me. I will go there alone.'

'Are you sure about it? I don't think you are optimistic about your decision. The way you were talking outside before, I doubt you are com...' Neha cut his voice and said:

'I did not come outside. I was here only.' Vikrant was not able to speak a word. It was horrendous.

'Are you lying?'

'Why would I lie? I am here from 2hours.' Vikrant had an unpleasant feeling of meeting a ghost. He thought it was Neha. *Ali disguised himself. He is filled with extremely dangerous wicked powers. Vikrant's detective was still alive.* Vikrant told her everything that happened outside in the lawn. Neha was equally shocked.

Only fear hung in the air. Only fear.

The past and the present are inseparable!

CHAPTER FOURTEEN

Kusum sat up, rubbing the sleep from her eyes. She was not feeling well. Her back was paining and due to cold she had a fever. She went inside the washroom and splashed some water on her face. Kusum was also worried about Neha. She did not want her to go to Jaipur. She wanted to stop her. Kusum knew Neha had very less chances to come back alive. But Neha had made up her mind. There was noise outside which grabbed Kusum's attention. She went in the drawing room. She was not able to spot anyone. She turned back to return in her room. She opened the door of her room and went inside, terrified. There were too many things going on in her mind when someone knocked the door of her room. This time she feared opening it. When she opened it, she saw a shadow moving here and there. Without wasting a second, she closed the door. Kusum was afraid of staying alone, now. She tried to call Neha. But her number was unreachable. "How's that possible? She's upstairs." Kusum shouted. Someone again, knocked the door. Kusum did not open the door. Kusum's hands were trembling because of the fear she was experiencing.

'Kusum aunty, open the door. I am Neha.' Kusum heard Neha's voice and almost jumped to open the door. Finally, Neha was inside the room. Kusum gave Neha a horror-stricken look.

'Why were you not responding?' asked Neha.

'I saw someone's shadow roaming in inside the house. I got afraid.' Neha hugged her to make her feel better.

'Why you came here?' Kusum asked trying to make an eye contact with Neha.

'I got your missed call. Just came to see if you need anything.' Neha said and released Kusum from her arms. She gave her a smile.

'Did you see anyone in the corridor?' Neha shook her head and smiled.

'Neha trust me, I am not lying. Believe me; I saw someone's shadow. Only shadow', Kusum mumbled. 'I understand, aunty. We all are living in fear. I know he has reached here to trouble us. Something happened with Vikrant sir, too.' Neha told her everything.

'This is horrifying. He has the power to transform himself into any one of us. Neha, I am telling you don't go there. He won't let you live there.'

'There is no point in arguing over the same topic again and again. I am going this is my final decision. That's all.' Neha declared. Kusum wanted her to be safe. But this time it was out of her control.

'How are you going to fight against him?'

'I don't know. I have not decided anything, yet.'

'Then decide something very fast. You're leaving tomorrow.' Kusum said and observed Neha. Neha looked lost. Neha murmured something to herself.

'What are you thinking?' Kusum asked her. Neha glared at Kusum.

'I am not thinking. I need some sleep. I am leaving tomorrow.' Neha said and got up to leave. Kusum closed the door behind her. Kusum came back to bed. Thoughts darted in Kusum's mind:

Neha, who wasn't sure about going to Jaipur, again is now foolishly going there. This has all happened after communicating with Ali's spirit. I don't know what she felt during those few minutes. I cannot let her go. But who is going to stop her. She is reckless, now. I just don't know?

Kusum's mind was full of worries and questions. She was tired. She wasn't taking Neha's decision too well. Questions continued flashing in her mind and there were no answers to any of them.

Suddenly, a voice from her mobile said, "The number you are trying to call is unreachable, please try again later". Kusum froze.

Kusum talked with Ali's spirit who disguised himself as Neha. Kusum had an unpleasant feeling of hugging an evil spirit. Someone knew Neha was leaving tomorrow.

Laughing time, it was.

CHAPTER FIFTEEN

Peter was in a pensive mood. Peter was trying to communicate with Ali's spirit. Peter wanted to ask him, what his motive was. Though, Neha had already told him everything. He did not trust Neha. The fact was, he did not trust anyone. He looked in the mirror thinking about Ali. Peter knew it was hard to call such an old spirit. Peter knew, the older they get, the more powerful they become. Their power is utterly devastating. There were very less chances of Ali's spirit communicating with Peter without the presence of Neha because Peter was not connected to Neha. But it happened. Tube lights dimmed. Peter closed his eyes. He did not want Ali's spirit to harm him. All he needed was a peaceful conversation with him, which was next to impossible.

'Why did you call me?' a voice whispered in Peter's ears. It is a good sign, Peter said to himself.

'I am a pious person. I don't have any problems regarding you on this earth. I only want to know why you are troubling that girl Neha. Why do you want to kill her?' Peter said, looking in the mirror. There was almost darkness inside the room. Peter's hands were shaking.

'Who are you to ask me this question?'

'I am a helper of god.' Peter said.

'God, who is he? I don't know anyone called god.' Blood rushed inside Peter's body. But Peter controlled himself. Peter ignored the note of disbelief in his voice.

'You did not answer me.'

'Why should I answer you? Who are you?' Voice became louder and clearer.

'I told you, who I am. I want to know why you are troubling her. That's all.'

'I'm going to finish her chapter from my life. I am going to kill her, soon.' Peter's ears couldn't believe it. *Finish her chapter.*

'I know about you, Ali. I know everything. Neha's grandfather killed you. She was not even born at that time when he killed you. What's her fault in all this?' Peter slightly opened his eyes. There was someone sitting in front of him. There was darkness in the room.

'Sometimes even if you are not at fault, you're punished. It was Alok's fault. He killed me. I will kill his whole family. Everyone, I vow.'

'What will you get by killing her?' Peter said. Peter knew evil spirits had feelings. He was trying to make him understand it was not right thing to do.

'Satisfaction' Ali's spirit said. 'I worship evil every day. He has given me powers which no person can understand. I am invincible.' There was a sound of laughing in the room. He roared with laughter. Peter's plan was not going well.

'No one is undefeatable.' Peter shouted at him. Suddenly, there was silence in the room.

'I am the king of darkness. No one has the power to defeat me.'

'I believe in my god. He has the power to defeat you and he will defeat you.'

'This is my revenge. I will take my revenge and this time. I will make sure I win.' Peter was surprised by his confidence. Peter opened his eyes. Lights were switched on. He felt light. Within a second, light switched off. He closed his eyes immediately.

'I promise Neha's death would be a great news.' Peter couldn't reply him. He had no answers. Peter tried to contact with god. He needed his help.

'I won't let anything happen to her. You're wrong, Ali.' Peter yelled.

'You can't do anything. You're a helpless and weak human.' *He is right what can I do, Peter thought.* Humans are weak and helpless. Ali was also a human, once. He was also a weak person, once and helpless one too. Evil spirits are powerful but angry than humans because there is a lot of negativity inside them. Good spirits are powerful but gratified because they have positivity filled in them.

'I will kill her I am going to end this story, very soon.' Ali said to Peter.

'Which story?' Peter asked Ali.

'The death story' Ali said and burst out laughing. For few minutes there was no noise. Peter assumed Ali's spirit left. That was something he wanted.

The death story, words echoed in Peter's mind.

For Neha, it was a new day with old problems fluttering over her mind. Neha was going to leave today. Neha was trying to prepare herself, mentally. She kept muttering in her mind, she has to be strong. She knew she was going to fight against an invisible and indomitable evil spirit. Neha, who never performed any prayers, today had god's name on her lips. Things were going to change. It can be against Neha or in favour of Neha. She kept reminding herself, she has to be strong. Today, she was a strong woman. She proved it. Women are strong, if given chance to prove themselves. It was 10 in the morning when Vikrant called Neha downstairs.

'Hello, I hope I am not disturbing you but this is about Ali.' Peter said to Neha. She sat on the sofa wondering why he had come to give her more tension.

'I contacted Ali's spirit pervious night.' Peter said everything about previous night to Neha. Kusum too told her about last night incident. Peter and Kusum both had experienced something evil. Neha tried to keep cool. Neha was not going to cancel her plan. Neha had decided it.

'I am telling you, Neha. He is very powerful. He can become exactly like you or me or anyone. He can fool you in seconds. Please, my child, don't go.' Kusum almost cried. Neha wasn't happy with whatever was going on. She wanted a ring of positivity around her but negative part was not letting it happen.

'I am going and no one is going to stop me.' Neha declared, once again.

'Trust me; Neha. Ali's spirit is deadly. We humans can never fight against him.' Neha was shocked by Peter's helplessness mood. She needed support and no one was ready to provide her that.

'Peter, you are saying it. You know what, I decided to go back because I thought humans are powerful than evil spirits. If you can call an evil spirit, a ghost or anything then why can't I get rid of him? I am going today and that's final.' Neha said. Peter took Neha's hand in his hands. Neha felt awkward.

'It isn't that way, Neha. There are energies in this world which are out of human control and understanding. Only god can understand it and fight against it. Let me explain you.' Peter said and tightened his grip on her hand. 'People do come in this world with conscious mind. But when they die, their body becomes lifeless. The consciousness which is left after death is a free. It can do anything and anyhow. We can't do anything about it, Neha.'

Neha looked into his eyes. Peter's eyes described only fear. It was a different kind of fear. It was fear of losing her. Neha pulled her hand back.

'That means we can never defeat his spirit.' Vikrant asked Peter.

'I will have to talk about this to the father of the church. He can tell me the solution.' Peter said, sharply.

'No! I am leaving today. I have to pack my bags too. See you, later.' Neha said and got up. Peter glanced at her. Neha did not look at Peter and walked without turning back. She closed the door and stood in front of the mirror.

I have no time for all this, Neha said to herself.

On the other hand, Peter felt an attachment towards Neha creeping over him. Well, he got his answer. Peter also understood Neha was a stubborn woman.

'Do you think she will be able to fight against Ali's spirit?' Vikrant asked.

'Future can never be predicted. What's her plan?'

'She's going alone and she says she has no plan.' Peter looked baffled.

'No plan' Peter said to himself.

CHAPTER SIXTEEN

Neha was lost. She was searching for someone who can help her. To her front, there were houses. They were beautiful. It was a town of only wooden houses. There were no people on the road. Neha was walking continuously from one hour. Her legs were paining. The bag in her hand was heavy. She did not understand why she was carrying that bag. Actually, she did not understand anything. She sat on a dusty bench. Her clothes too were dirty. She wanted rest. She looked here and there. There was no one. Neha stood up and started walking towards her right, again. Neha spotted a man who was walking near a house. She called out for him. He stopped and looked at her. Neha went up to him. He smiled at her.

'I think I am lost. Can you get me out of here?' Neha asked him. He smiled at her and told her to follow him. He stopped near a house. 'Wait here. I will come in two minutes.' He said and went inside a wooden house. Neha stood there. There was peace there. He did not come for

next five minutes. Restless and thirsty Neha knocked at the same door, he had walked in few minutes ago. This time someone else opened the door. He was an old man, with a black beard. His eyes were sparkling and he was simply dressed.

'Yes! May I help you?' The man who opened the door said.

'A man came inside this house. He was going to help me moving out of this place.' Neha said, and biting her lower lip. He smiled.

'I don't think if someone came inside. I think you're mistaken. I stay here alone.' The man answered. After hearing his answer, Neha had a serious expression on her face. She was been completely fooled by an old man. She saw that man going inside. She knew he was lying.

'What? I saw him entering this house. Uncle, I am already irritated. Please help me.' Neha pleaded.

'I see you you're tired and you need some rest. Come inside.' He said and Neha blindly stepped inside. He gave her a full glass of water.

'How you came here?' He asked Neha.

'I don't know. I don't remember anything. I am blank.' She answered. The house of the old man was clean. 'By the way, what is this place?'

'This is my kingdom.' Neha laughed at his answer. He joined her.

'What kind of kingdom is it? There are no people. What is name of this kingdom?' Neha asked him.

'This is called as God's kingdom and there are people here.' His words had to spring Neha's attention. Neha's hands started shaking. 'Open the door and look outside.' Neha opened the door and saw there were people roaming

around. They were all smiling. They were all happy. Shocked Neha was sure about one thing—she was with god. Neha turn around and saw that man she laughed on was still smiling. Neha went and touched his feet for his blessings. He hugged Neha.

'I am here. Am I...dead?' Neha asked, stammering.

'No. You're here because you have some problems in life. You look at that bag.' Neha looked at the bag she was carrying.

'What problems?' Neha questioned.

'You don't remember anything because your problems are in that bag. No one can come to me with their problems.'

'Why people cannot come here with their problems?'

'There are certain rules I have set. I make people follow them.' Neha looked down. She was feeling guilty about asking such a question to god.

'Don't worry, Neha. I am god but firstly I am your friend. Treat me as your friend.' Neha smiled. She looked into his sparkling eyes; she was able to see the entire universe.

'Neha, take this bag.' God said and handed her the bag. 'Open it. You will remember everything.' Neha opened the bag. In minutes, she remembered everything. Neha looked at god with strained face.

'Neha, you know I created one type of power and actually now there are two types of powers existing.' Neha was confused.

'I created one power that is called—human power. And humans created the second power which is known as—evil power. I will tell how this evil power was created. I created a man and gave him a brain to think. I told him, if he works daily I will give him food, every day. For some

years, he worked every day and I gave him food. One day, he did not complete his work. When I came to meet him, he told me, he won't work for me. I did not give him food that day. Next day, when I came to meet him, I saw he had created another power using his power of thinking. That is how evil power was born in the world. I only created humans. Humans created evilness in my world.' God said. 'I killed that man. But the power he created never left...'

'Why I am here?' Neha asked god. It was a direct question from her.

'I will answer you.' god said to Neha.

'Did you see wooden houses outside?' Neha agreed.

'This is heaven. People after spending their life on the earth come here. I have given everyone their own house to live, peacefully. That is why there is silence here.' Neha did not understand what god means to say?

'Come let's go for a walk.'

They were both standing near a lake. Neha was constantly observing a thing. She wanted ask him something.

'Do you see that house?' God said, pointing towards a house hardly visible due to fog.

'Yes.'

'It is your house and it is under construction. It will take me years to construct it. I am a lone worker.' He said and smiled. Neha smiled too.

'Don't be afraid, Neha. No one can decide anyone's death, except me.' Neha was filled with confidence. She knew she was going to defeat the evil spirit who was troubling her.

'I know. I know.' Neha said.

'You won't remember anything, Neha. Later, after leaving from here, you won't remember anything whatever I have said to you.' Neha looked at god with hopeful eyes. Neha did not know anything about how she was going to fight against Ali's spirit. Neha was observing something from a very long time.

'How will I fight against him, alone?' Neha asked god.

'I don't know. I cannot reveal the future to you. You will have to live it on your own.'

'I don't understand.' Neha said.

'It's your time to go back, Neha. I hope you do good things in life.' God said. Neha was speechless.

'Whenever dark thoughts come in your mind, just remember one simple thing: only brightness can defeat darkness.' God said, lastly.

CHAPTER SEVENTEEN

Riya checked her watch for the fifth time. She was waiting for Suresh to come. Mukesh, Riya's husband was also standing with her. Riya disclosed everything to Mukesh. Riya feared going to Neha's house alone with Suresh, it was not because she did not trust him; it was only because Mukesh gave her confidence and relief to her heart. A sense of protection, she felt with Mukesh. Suresh arrived. His face said everything. He was not happy to see Mukesh with Riya.

'I am sure. Neha is in danger. We need to go inside their house.' Suresh said, running a hand through his hair.

'Ashish is also inside that house and you said he is no more. This is damn crazy.' Mukesh said and laughed at his own joke. He seriously, never believed in supernatural powers. He just came with Riya to protect her.

'This is not crazy. Neha's life can be at stake. The problem is how are we going to get inside?' Riya almost shouted at Mukesh. Suresh wanted to laugh, but he did not.

'Let's go there, first.'

The silences in nights are the most frightening ones. Riya, Suresh and Mukesh were experiencing it. After the deadly encounter with Ashish, Riya was afraid of staying alone at home. They moved inside slowly trying to make no noise. They saw the door was locked. Suresh went on the rear side to see if any window was open or not. He came back with a negative response. None of them talked. They were all in fear and trepidation.

'There's only one way to go inside.' Riya and Mukesh looked at Suresh as if he were a genius. Suresh picked up a medium sized stone from the ground and hurled it on the window. The smash was hard and the glass window was in pieces. He smiled at Riya and Mukesh. They were not happy, though. It was not the way but ideas from Suresh were always out of the box. They all jumped inside.

They saw no change in the house. The house was neat and clean. They switched on the lights.Suresh and Mukesh went upstairs to find Neha while Riya was busy observing the atmosphere, downstairs. Riya looked around. She went near the shelf and saw a book fallen down. She picked up. While keeping the book back, a note fell from it.

She collected it and read: "Don't come here".

Riya felt as if a voice yelled in her ears. She plunged the note, there itself and stepped back.

Suresh and Mukesh came down. They shook their heads. There was no one upstairs. Riya knew only one place was left to look after. That was—the store room. Riya opened the door of the store room and saw a dead body. The dead body of Ashish. She screamed.

'I told you, he's dead.' Riya yelled, looking at Mukesh. He looked horrified. They had never seen a dead body in their life. It was their first time.

'Stop the drama. Look at this.' Suresh said and pointed at the knife on the floor. Suddenly, there was a noise. It seemed like someone was laughing. Riya and Mukesh both held each other's hands. Suresh moved closer to them. Automatically, store room's door closed. They looked at each other with horror in their eyes. Something very wrong was going on. Laughing stopped. There was no sound for a minute.

Mukesh went near the door and opened it. Meanwhile a shadow passed by Riya. She screamed in horror.

'Why are you screaming?' Mukesh asked.

'I... saw someone's shadow.' Riya said stammering. She was blank. Words were not coming out from their mouth. They heard police sirens while running towards the main door. All of them stopped on the spot. Within two minutes, one police inspector and two police constables were inside the house.

'What are you doing here?' asked the police inspector to three of them.

'We came here to meet our friend.' Mukesh lied. Police inspector told his constables to search every corner of the house. They were all afraid. They did not know how police came here? Their brain had stop working.

'What is the name of your friend?'

'Neha' replied Riya.

'A girl' inspector said and gave her a smile. She did not like it. The fact was each one of them was shocked. One constable called out for the inspector. He told, Riya,

Suresh and Mukesh to follow him. They went in the store room.

'There is dead body here.' The constable said.

'So, she is your friend.' The inspector said pointing towards the dead body. Riya was feeling giddiness. Mukesh and Suresh had no answers. The inspector continued to blame three of them and his constable took notes. Riya felt giddy. She was about to fall down. Her head was paining. Before tumbling down, she saw something. She was shocked to see it.

Riya saw, the year written on the note pad was 1972...

CHAPTER EIGHTEEN

"Once you go inside your house, don't think of coming back. He won't let you, come back. He is ready and knows everything already." –Vikrant said to Neha before leaving.

Neha got down at Jaipur railway station after a hectic journey. She had fever, and needed some rest before going to her house. But she had no option. Neha did not want to meet people around her. Her mind required silence. Anyways, by night she was going to enter the house. Neha couldn't think of heading back. She had promised everyone, she would come alive or she would die. These were the two options left with her. A call on her mobile came, disturbing her thoughts. It was from her aunty.

'Neha, are you safe?' These were Kusum's first words. Neha was touched. She was the one who had always helped her in life and was helping her in the present as well.

'I just reached. I am just trying to figure out things.' Neha replied.

'Do you want to come back?'

'I am not even thinking about it. My decision is final. Anyways, did he come again?' Neha was asking about Ali's spirit. She wanted check if he is still troubling them, there.

'No. We are fine. Go to a temple or a church before moving inside. Take god's blessings. Should I come there?'

'No I am okay. Kusum aunty, take care of Vikrant sir. I will be coming soon.' Neha wanted to add "if possible".

'Neha… I want to…' Neha could hear Kusum was almost in tears.

'You want to what?'

'Nothing' Kusum declined. 'Best of luck'

'Thank you! I am switching off my mobile. I don't want anyone to disturb me.' Neha said. Before Kusum would say anything, Neha disconnected the call.

Kusum was feeling weak. Kusum wanted to tell Neha about it. She tried. Vikrant came inside her room and asked:

'You told her the truth.'

'I did not. She is still unknown to the truth.' Kusum hissed.

'You should have told her.'

'I know.' Kusum said.

Neha checked in to a hotel nearby. Neha freshen her up. She ordered a coffee for herself. She sat up cross-legged on the bed. She was thinking about how to go about Ali. Of course, she had decided that she was not going to take anyone with her. She was going to her house alone. She didn't want anyone to get hurt just because of her problem. Neha was thinking about how Ali's spirit would attack her. He can also kill her wasting no time. But the fact was; Ali did not like playing with his victims.

Neha was going to be his favorite victim. Neha knew it was going to be threatening. She knew there is a weak side of everyone. Ali's spirit must also have a weak side. Neha knew he would not possess her again. Ali would do something very different from all his wicked acts. Neha had not made any plan to defeat him. She only wanted to go and face whatever fate had stored for her. In her case, fate was always strange, indeed.

Neha had forgiven everyone in her life, except one person. Though, Neha had forgotten about Alok's mistake but she had not forgiven him. She just could not forgive him. Just because of her grandfather her love died. That also by her hand. The reason behind all her sufferings was—Alok. Neha, somewhere inside her heart she knew, she would never forgive Alok.

It was near to 5pm in the evening. More 3 hours and Neha would be in her haunted house, again. With every passing minute, Neha was getting more and more perturbed. There was nothing she could do. She was deprived of sleep. She got up from the bed and pulled out her diary from her bag. She took a pen in her and started writing:

> What I can't tell to anyone I write it here! There's nothing much left to write. I am in a big pool with problems around me. I can't swim. There's no one around me to help me, too.
>
> Ali has mysterious powers in him. To defeat him, I will also need mysterious powers. That is why I need magic in my life.

Magic, is what Neha needed in her life. "I can't let myself engross in emotions." Neha reminded herself again.

Riya woke up with a sudden jerk. Riya's body was paining. She was on the bed, inside her home. She saw Mukesh watching her.

'Mukesh, how come I am here? We were at that house.' Riya said, touching her forehead. She realized her head was aching and she also had fever.

'When I and Suresh came from upstairs we saw you lying on the floor. What happened there?'

Riya squeezed her forehead trying to remember things.

'We went to the store room and discovered his body. Police came, on? Someone was laughing.' Riya said, one by one. 'Yes! I remember everything. Listen…' Riya told him about Ashish's dead body, someone laughing, shadow and the police enquiry. Mukesh was shocked to hear, everything. Whatever happened with Riya was not reality. It was a dream. A bad dream, Riya thought.

'I saw something written on the note pad. It was written—1972.' Riya said, excited.

'What does it mean?' Mukesh questioned.

'1972, year it can be.'

'What about it?'

'I don't know. Something of that sort must have happened there in the year 1972. I mean murder of someone.' Riya guessed. Riya coughed and sneezed. Mukesh could not take it anymore. He did not want Riya to be unhealthy just because of some random cases around them. He supported her but her health was his first priority.

'Take some rest, Riya. There's a lot of time remaining to discuss all this.'

'Mukesh, I have just got up. By the way what's the time?'

'I don't want to tell you.' Mukesh said. Riya made a face and switched on her mobile.

The time was 6.30 in the evening. Riya had slept non-stop for 19 hours. Riya was in tears. Mukesh hugged her tightly. Riya was crying. Mukesh tried to console her.

'Mukesh, I really don't know…' Riya had no words. 19 hours had struck her hard. 19 hours, Mukesh was sitting beside Riya. Mukesh was praying for her to regain consciousness.

'I know. Just relax. Everything will be okay.' Mukesh assured her.

'I can't relax until I see Neha. She is a very good girl, Mukesh. I have to find Neha. Things are not going right. She can be in trouble.' Riya blurted.

'Some things are not in our hands, darling.' Mukesh said to her. Riya was hyperventilating under stress and Mukesh did not want her to be stressed.

'You mean Neha is also dead.'

'I did not say that. I am only trying to say, we cannot take a torch and search for Neha. It will not make any sense.' Mukesh said.

'But Mukesh' Mukesh silenced her with a kiss.

There was no time to romance. Mukesh kissed her, just to silence her. Riya quietly moved away with a smile on her face. Riya closed the washroom door and tried to divert her mind.

In this case, negative powers were stronger than positive ones. Everyone knew it. No one wanted to believe it.

CHAPTER NINETEEN

He was crying. He knew he had done no wrong. He was right. People supported him and actually loved him for killing him. The person he had killed—was a murderer who had murdered many people.

He felt his own family was against him. He wanted to prove it to them. How will he? He was worried about her. She was blaming him for all her problems. He knew it was not right. He wanted to cry more. He was hurt by her decisions. There were things she was still unaware of. He wanted to reveal it to her. He was helpless. He looked at himself. He was old but he was a good person. He believed in god. God had helped him. He was grateful to god. It was going to be tough to come in front of her. He was her savior but she was unknown to it.

He tried to put a smile on his face. He was free.

Neha was standing in front of her house thinking whether to go inside or not? Neha knew there was no point in turning back. There was a different kind of atmosphere out there. Neha did not want to go at the back side. That is where she had buried Ashish's dead body. Neha didn't want to think about Ashish but she was helplessly thinking about him.

'Neha' a voice from her right side came. It was Riya. She was happy to see Neha safe. Neha was not at all happy to see Riya. She knew Riya would ask her a million questions.

'Hello' Neha replied, softly.

'It's not safe to be here. Let's go inside my house.' Riya said immediately and almost hauled Neha inside her house. Neha had no option. She will have to answer some of her questions.

Mukesh got up from the sofa as he saw Neha inside her house. Mukesh instantly liked her. Neha like always looked beautiful. Riya gave a glass of water to her and sat with her.

'Actually, I was on vacation. Ashish is still in Shimla. I came back.' Neha tried to explain.

'Ashish's dead. We know it.' Riya said.

Neha felt numb. She couldn't speak, anymore.

'Neha, are you okay?' Riya asked. Neha shook her head. Neha was not feeling well. She was feeling worst.

'How do you know it?' Riya told her everything. What she saw, she heard, everything only skipping the dream part. Riya felt it was irrelevant. Mukesh sat there listening to them. Neha was shocked. "Ali's spirit used Ashish's body to scare her." Neha said to herself.

'Where were you all these days? I was so worried. Suresh too was worried about you.' Neha had decided she won't tell anything to anyone. Some things demand secrecy.

'Riya, I can't answer any of your questions. I have to go home.' Neha said. Riya got furious.

'Are you nuts'? You know there is someone inside that bloody house who is killing people. Still I am hearing it from you. Why you want to go in that haunted house?' Riya yelled.

'It is my house, Riya. I can't leave my house just because of horror.'

'Do you think she needs a psychiatrist?' Riya said looking at Mukesh. He did not respond. 'Listen, I don't want any more deaths in this colony. I can't let you go there. It is haunted.'

'Let it be haunted. I don't care. No one can stop me from going there. It's my house and on my land.' Neha said, angrily. She got up to leave.

'Why are you behaving like this?'

'Like what?'

'Like a madwoman.' Riya said. It reminded Neha of Ali. He also murdered people wearing a mask of a madman. But he wasn't mad.

'Riya, silence won't end it. The only person who can end it is—me.' Neha wanted to say more but stopped herself.

'I don't understand it. How will you do that?' Riya asked.

'I don't know.' Neha cooed. Riya gave her a glare. 'But I will figure out' She added. Neha was feeling bad. She did not want to hurt or argue with Riya regarding it. Neha knew Riya cared for her.

'Is there something I don't know? Are you hiding something?'

Neha shook her head and said, 'I think I should leave. Thanks for worrying about me.'

'Wait! We should complaint in police about Ashish. Someone has killed him.' This time Mukesh said. Neha's heart was almost in pieces.

'You cannot see that someone... Mr' Neha answered. She knew she can be in jail if police comes and investigates. "Riya should not ask about Ashish's cremation", Neha thought.

'Well, I don't know anything about seen or unseen. I think it is better to inform police. They can help us.' Mukesh and took out his mobile.

'What if it kills them too?' Neha said in a firm voice. There was confidence in her voice.

'What?' Riya and Mukesh both said in unison.

'Yes. Anything can happen, Riya. Anything' Neha said and left.

Riya and Mukesh sat there wondering what was going to happen. They tried stopping Neha but she did not listen to them. She was going to enter her house. Many scary things were going to happen.

Neha was again standing in front of her haunted house. Ali's spirit also resided there. Neha pushed the rust-covered Iron Gate. Neha saw plants she had planted were dead because of lack of water. Neha bend down and touched them. She loved planting. There were many thoughts bouncing in her mind. Neha unlocked the door of her house. It was like opening door for her death. *My death story, she thought*. She switched on the lights and fan.

Neha sat on the sofa and flexed her hands. She thought of making tea for her. There was silence. She was not thinking about Ashish or Ali. She had prepared herself, mentally. Neha was mentally prepared to deal with whatever was going to happen. It was late night but she decided not to sleep. She went to bedroom and changed her clothes. She got busy with her other works.

It was time to meet her destiny.

'I am worried about her. If something happens to her, I won't be able to forgive myself.' He said to himself. She had to identify him before she meets him otherwise it can lead to her death. Many things were happening at a same time. Tension and fear hung in the air.

It was going to be a horrid night.

CHAPTER TWENTY

Someone was calling Neha just to let her know she is safe. At the same time, someone was calling Neha just to let her know, her life was going to end soon. She could hear only one of them. Someone was wandering around her. It was Ali's spirit. Ali wanted to hit her. Ali wanted to show her, he is the best and he is immortal. It was his chance to take revenge.

Neha slowly moved inside the store room and opened an old cupboard placed there. There were some documents kept in it. She removed them and cleaned the dirt on it. She sat there reading it. Those were Alok's case files. She wanted to read every case, he had solved. Neha was busy reading those files when someone applying little amount of force pulled her hair. She did not react. She assumed nothing has happened and continued reading further. After some time she went to the drawing room. Neha wasn't afraid of anyone, this time. She quietly sat on the sofa reading every single page written. There were almost over 1000 pages. Her mobile rang. She looked. The screen displayed an unknown number. Neha understood—Ali's spirit was trying to divert her mind. Neha promised Kusum she would switch off her mobile but she intentionally kept it on She wanted to irritate someone.

Two hours passed, it was 2am. Neha began yawning. She was feeling sleepy. But she had option but to stay awake. Her life was at stake. *No danger, yet, she thought.*

Danger was on its way. She picked up another page from the case files and read in her mind: 'Ali—serial killings.' Next moment, lights went off! There was darkness around her. It was her time to step into the dark world. Neha got up and tried not to worry about it. She was on her way towards her bedroom when she noticed footsteps following her. She turned around. There was only darkness. Neha switched on the torch. Neha knew Ali would try to do something different. She sat on the bed wondering what was going to happen next!

"Please! Help me! I want to help her." Someone was shouting. Fact was: no one was able to hear him.

Some force pushed Neha hard. She fell on the floor. She got up and sat up again. Neha using her torch looked here and there. Neha could feel as if someone was watching her in the room. Neha closed her eyes. She was trying to relax when she heard some noise of heavy melt falling down from a height. Neha got up and went to the kitchen to see if something has fallen. Nothing was fallen. Neha wondered what that sound was of? Neha's mobile rang, again. Neha decided to ignore it.

"Neha" someone whispered in her ears. Neha turned to look back and saw a middle aged man standing her front of her. Neha screamed. She almost got a heart attack. He was looking straight into her eyes. Neha rooted on the spot. Neha had no guts to move an inch. Suddenly, he disappeared. Neha wanted to cry.

"Don't cry. Be strong." Neha said to herself and took a deep breath.

"Neha" again, someone whispered. Ali was trying to scare her. Ali wanted to throw her into panic so that he would get hold of her. Neha was prepared for his old techniques. Constantly, in her mind, she was repeating her mantra.

'I don't fear you, Ali. I know who you're and why are you troubling me. I am not afraid of you.' Neha shouted in full volume. Ali's spirit pushed her on the sofa and said:

"Shush! Don't worry. I will kill you tonight. I don't like to waste time, Neha." Ali's spirit said.

'I will kill you. I will...' Neha was talking; Ali suddenly broke in.

"No one can kill me. I am deathless and your death is near, Neha. Be afraid. Be very afraid, Neha."

'I am not afraid of you, Ali. It's your revenge, right? Then I can also take revenge. You killed my husband.' Neha yelled at him. Neha tried to get up. She was not able to. She stayed there as if someone had glued her on sofa.

"I don't like to hear, jokes! Alok killed me. I killed his whole family. It is only you who is left." Ali said.

Neha thought of her Kusum aunty.

'You're right, evil. I am the only person left.' Neha said, hesitating.

"Are thinking about your Kusum aunty?" Ali said and laughed. *He knows what I thought few seconds back, Neha noticed.*

"She is not your real aunt. You don't have blood-relation with her. Kusum was adopted by Alok." Ali said, happily.

'You're lying' Neha said. Ali's spirit did not respond. He was only laughing. *Why would he lie?*

Neha went into a state of shock. The woman who took care of her was not related to her by blood. All the while, Kusum didn't even reveal it to her. Well, there are relationships in this world which are more than just blood.

He had succeeded in diverting Neha's mind. Something was coming for Neha. Something.

Neha felt weak. Something in her was dying. It was hope and faith. Neha closed her eyes. Ali's laugh was still audible. It was getting louder with every passing minute. Neha's face grew sadder and Ali's confidence increased. Neha had no tricks to defeat Ali. *I came here to end my life. Just because I was tired of it, thoughts shuffled in Neha's mind.*

There must be something I am missing, she said to herself.

"Are you ready to die?" He asked her.

'Eh?'

"I asked, are you ready to die?" Ali asked her again. Neha look down. She had no answer.

"I'd assume you are ready." He said loudly.

He was cursing himself. He was not able to do anything. He was going to watch her death. He came here to save her. She read about him. She did not remember him once. Her hatred for him was limitless.

He was worried and nervous. He was also afraid.

Please call me, he thought.

Invisible Ali dragged Neha till the store room. Neha's back was paining. Ali was enjoying her pain. Suddenly, tube light in the store room switched on, automatically. Neha saw a hammer placed in front of her. Neha's face described the fear in her mind. It was Ali's favourite weapon. He used hammer to kill people, earlier.

"Alok killed me, here. This was his drawing room years ago. I still remember how he fired bullets on me? That day, I vowed, I won't let him or his family live peacefully. I want to end it here, where it all started!" Ali said. Neha came here to kill him and not to be killed by him. But Neha's end was near.

"Let's end it here, then" Neha said and laughed.

Her death is near! Her death is near! He was hollering inside the house. He was afraid and helpless. One chance, and I will make everything alright, he begged. All he wanted was that one chance.

Neha stopped laughing and got up. This time she was able to. She looked around and started laughing again. She felt like a lunatic. All her fears transformed into madness. She was going to die. She knew it. But she couldn't escape from it. Suddenly, Neha's eyes welled up! She began to cry. Neha cried while Ali rejoiced. Neha closed her eyes when she received a stroke of the hammer on her leg. She screamed in pain. She did not open her eyes and sat there sobbing. Ali smacked her face, hard. Blood started flowing from her nose.

'Neha relax. There should be some way out.' Someone inside her said.

'I don't think so. He is going to kill me with the hammer. I am already bleeding.' Neha said.

'Don't worry. Think of something. There is a way to defeat him. You need to find it. I have done my job. Bye.'

Neha saw someone in front of her. She couldn't' believe it. Ali pressed her face on the floor and suddenly the hammer was flying in the air. *One minute is remaining, Neha fast, she said to herself.*

Neha openedher eyes. There was darkness around her. "It's your time to die." Ali said.

'Only brightness can defeat darkness' Neha said to herself observing the darkness around her.

Brightness! Who can bring brightness in my dark life? Fast Neha, only twenty seconds are remaining.

Neha could feel someone standing behind her holding the hammer. He was going to hit her, hard.

'Grandpa was the one who killed Ali previously.' Neha said, loudly. 'Grandpa'

Neha opened her eyes. Hammer disappeared. But there was still darkness. There was still someone standing behind her holding something in his hand. This time, it was her grandfather, Alok. She went outside the store room. Swiftly temperature inside the house, decreased. Neha went in the drawing and saw a man standing there. She was not able to identify him due to lack of light. He had something in his hand. Automatically, lights turned on. The man standing in front of her had a pistol in his hand. He pointed the pistol towards her and fired a bullet. Neha ducked and noticed there was another man standing behind her with a hammer in his hand. Neha looked at him. He was Ali. He was in pain and was muttering something in a low voice. Then who was the one she saw in front of her?

Neha turned around. There he was. Alok Rajput, her grandfather. They both looked at each other. He was the same person she hated the most. He saved her. He was her saviour. He was her hero. He had to go back. He knew it. He had come on the earth to complete one incomplete chapter of his life. Suddenly, he disappeared leaving something.

Neha stood there. No thoughts were running in her mind. Neha did not want to think anything. She was feeling happy. She was tension free. There was brightness around her and there was brightness in her life too.

Neha lost her husband in this battle. She also gained out of it. It was her faith in her.

Neha looked forward and smiled.

CHAPTER TWENTY ONE

There is no life without problems and challenges. Life is tough. Neha had learned it. She had faced problems in her childhood. She also faced problems as a teenager. Always, problems followed her. Problems and pain was her companion. Pain she suffered was unbearable. Yet, she did not give up and did not let hope die. She had a problematic life but it was a thrilling one.

'You have done it, Neha. You survived.' Kusum said, joyfully. Vikrant and Kusum had come to meet Neha in Jaipur. It was tough for Vikrant but he managed to travel. After all, her grand-daughter had defeated an evil spirit. No one took Ali's name and continued talking about various things.

'Neha, I want to tell you something.' Kusum said in middle of some conversation. Neha and Vikrant looked at her. Neha knew what she was going to say. Ali had already disclosed that thing to her.

'Please don't. I know and I think it is a white lie. You're my Kusum aunty. Please don't say anything.' Neha said with faith for Kusum in her eyes.

'But Neha…'

'Please, I said, change the topic… Same old stories I don't like.' Neha said and got up to go to kitchen.

'This girl is very smart. She won't let you feel pain. She will absorb it.' Vikrant said after Neha left. Kusum's eyes got wet. Happy times had come. Happy tears they were.

'Today's dinner will be special.' Neha shouted happily.

Perhaps, Neha was happy. But she knew she would not love anyone, again.

They finished their dinner and Neha was sitting on the sofa looking towards the shelf. Vikrant walked in and asked Neha: 'What are you looking at?'

'Grandpa was great. I read his case files. I mean those are yours too. He had written about everything in it. How the murder happened? Struggles, emotions, murders, and murderers, all he has written. Ali's case was not the hardest one but it was tricky and misleading. I just wonder why I became so selfish. He was not a selfish man. In fact, he saved people. I don't deserve to be called as his grand-daughter. Shame on me' Neha said almost in tears.

'Don't say that. You're brave. You fought for survival. That's what one should do. Be proud of yourself.'

'Grandpa, I have decided something. I'm leaving this house, forever.'

'No one will buy this house, ever. People still think it is haunted.'

I won't sell this house. This house was Ashish's dream.' Neha stopped for a minute and added. 'Can I come with you?'

'You don't have to ask. Just come along with me tomorrow. I know many horrible memories are attached to this house and it will haunt you. You don't have to suffer anymore.'

'That is why I have made this decision.' Neha said. They both were talking when Kusum walked in. Neha smiled at her. Kusum wanted to discuss an important thing with Neha and Vikrant. It was about Neha's marriage.

'Neha, you still have your whole life in front of you. I am thinking about your marri...'

'Marriage' Neha exclaimed. Neha was hurt by it.

'Don't get me wrong but you cannot stay alone. You need a life partner.'

'Why can't I stay alone? Actually, I am not alone. Ashish may have died but his soul still wanders around me. He will always be my husband. He will always hold a special place in my heart and no one can win that place other than him. So, it is better not to talk about it.' Neha said.

'I was only giving it a try'

'Some things never change, Kusum aunty.' Neha said lastly. There was silence for a minute.

'I have my own case file but still I want to read Alok's case file. Can you please pass it to me?' Vikrant said breaking the silence. Neha nodded and got up to give the file. Vikrant opened it and saw a paper in it. It looked like it was new sheet. He opened it.

'See, what I have got.' Vikrant called out for Kusum and Neha.

'What?'

'Alok's letter' He left something before leaving.

'Read it for us, Neha.' Vikrant handed her the paper. Neha began to read.

Dear Neha,

I know you hate me. I understand it. I shouldn't have gifted you that land but I had no option. Before dying I wrote a letter and gave it to Vikrant. I should have told you about it, earlier. I had chances but I did not. I was afraid. What if you back off? I thought. I kept it secret because I wanted me family's legacy to continue. I wasn't selfish. I was only protective towards my family's future. My mistake shouldn't spoil anyone else's life. I knew my past was going ruin my family's future.

Sometimes we trick our children just to let them know the truth. I am sorry for that.

I won't make it a long letter.

I love you all and a special thanks to Vikrant. And if possible forgive me Neha.

It won't give you anything.

Alok Rajput

Neha thought for a moment.
'I am adopting a child.' Neha said.
Vikrant smiled at her and Kusum too was happy.
Someone somewhere up was also happy.

WHAT HAPPENED AFTERWARDS?

'Come here you're late.' Neha shouted at him.

'I am not going to school. I have a headache.' He said.

'You're alright! These are all your drama.' Neha said trying to pull him out of his bed.

'Please, mom. I promise I will study at home today.' Neha smiled. She loved his drama.

'Okay. Last time I am leaving you. Tomorrow you are going to school without uttering a word.' He smiled and gave her kiss. 'Wake up soon, Ashish.' She said and left his room.

Neha named her adopted son—Ashish. Neha lives in Shimla. She takes home tuitions, now.

Neha is happy with Ashish. Maybe god planned her life that way just to give an orphan a shelter and love.

Vikrant's health is not so good these days. But he is happy to have someone in his life. But his days of loneliness are behind him.

Kusum too shifted with Neha to Vikrant's house and they both look after Vikrant.

Neha did not tell anything to Riya. She is still confused. Anyways, Mukesh loves Riya, unconditionally. Their life is settled.

Suresh continues to shout at his wife for not preparing breakfast on time. Neha met Suresh before leaving for Shimla. But he is still not aware of anything related to Ali.

What about Neha's house?

Well, someone is sitting on the chair and typing something. He is busy. He is typing his autobiography for himself. He can't publish it nor can anyone read it other than him. He has almost completed typing it. Only one last chapter is remaining. He is thinking about an appropriate title for his last chapter. He thinks about something and types: The Death Story.

EPILOGUE

'I have never heard anything like this.' I said. She smiled at me. She understood I liked it. It was already—6.30. Mumbai was about to come. I was having boring journey but somehow this woman made it special by telling me this story.

'So, you liked it?'

'Like is not the word. I loved it. But it is not a true one, right?'

'Of course this story is true. It depends on you, if you want to believe or not. I told you this story just to pass time.' She said with a smile on her face.

'There are too many unrealistic incidents in the story. Wait! I am missing something. You told me, you would scare me by telling me this story. See, I am not afraid. In fact, I am happy.' I said laughing. She laughed with me.

'Why are you laughing?' I asked.

'I am laughing at myself.' She said. I looked at her trying to know what she must be thinking.

'That's weird.'

'I am weird.' She said. This is strange. I realized she was not mature. She was mad. I kept quiet waiting for this journey to end. It was a memorable journey, though.

'Why were you saying you are a spirit?' I asked.

'Just to scare you' why is she so interested in scaring me?

'Why do you want to scare me?' I questioned.

'Because that's what we do.' I was puzzled. I did not ask her anything after that.

'Who did you like in the story? Any specific character' she asked me and drank a sip of water.

'Vikrant. He is like me.'

'One who decides to stay alone?'

'Correct! I don't like to socialize. I am a homebody.' I said.

'Anyways, I think our journey has almost ended. I can see the station.' I turned around to look at the station. Silently, we got down. She did not speak nor I. Still I wanted to tell her something but I did not. We waved goodbyes and went to different directions.

I looked for a taxi. I could not help myself thinking about my mysterious encounter with Nita. Who she was? Why she wanted to scare me? I was tired but she was all over my mind. The story she told me was also a rare one. Was she Neha?

'Stop thinking about it, Amay' I scolded myself.

I climbed up two floors. When I was opening the door, my neighbor opened his door and said:

'Here are your newspapers. Every day he came and delivered it. They were all lying on the floor.' We forgot to

tell our newspaper vendor about our holidays. I took the newspapers with me and went inside.

I started reading one of those newspapers. I was on the fourth page. I saw the woman's photo I met on the train in a corner. Headlines written below her photo frightened me.

"A Woman Killed In a Car Accident"

She was really a spirit. I became anxious. I really met a ghost while travelling on a train. Oh shit! On doubt she was laughing at herself. I was confused, why did she tell me that story? Why me?

She wanted to scare me. She wanted to me to fear. No! This is not making any sense, I shouted. I am a writer and she is ghost, there is no connection. She told me a story. No correction: she told me her story.

Yes! Her story.

Printed in the United States
By Bookmasters